BOB WAR & POKE

HARVEY WATSON

Houghton Mifflin Company
Boston   1991

Library of Congress Cataloging-in-Publication Data

Watson, Harvey.
  Bob War and Poke / by Harvey Watson.
    p. cm.
  Summary: Delighted to be hired as chauffeur and cook to a rich couple passing through town, two young brothers from the country have many adventures until they discover that their employers are bank robbers and thieves.
  ISBN 0-395-57038-7
  [1. Crime and criminals—Fiction. 2. Voyages and travels—Fiction. 3. Brothers—Fiction. 4. Country life—Fiction.]
  I. Title.
PZ7.W3269Bo   1991   90-26202
[Fic]—dc20   CIP
                  AC

Chapter 2 of this book appeared in slightly altered format in *Cricket*.

Printed in the United States of America
BP 10 9 8 7 6 5 4 3 2 1

This book is dedicated to my wife, Linda Kay,
for her love and understanding,
to Allen Lankton for his technical advice,
and to Jane Rolf for typing the manuscript.

CHAPTER
1

The sheriff handcuffed Ralph to one arm of the deputy and me to his other arm. The deputy was a big man, stern faced and slow moving. He was so tall, I barely came to his belt buckle.

They handcuffed Clutter and ran a chain through the handcuffs down to his leg shackles. When they had secured us, a deputy opened the cell door, and we all followed the sheriff out of the jailhouse into the bright sunlight.

The sheriff led the way across the street to the town square. Clutter shuffled along in his leg shackles behind him, and behind Ralph, the deputy, and me was a guard with a shotgun. We made our way down the brick sidewalk to the courthouse.

Outside the limestone building, some old men sat talking on a park bench. They stopped their chatter and stared at us as we passed. One of them whispered "bank robbers" to his companions. In front of the entrance, a group of men lounged around the double doors. One of the men was Freck.

It was good to recognize a friendly face for a change. Freck grinned at me and raised his hand as a greeting.

"Hi, Bob War," he said to me as I approached. "I got a chance to talk to the sheriff about you-all."

"Thanks," I answered as the tall deputy pulled me along. The sheriff entered the courtroom.

"Just tell them the truth, boy!" Freck yelled at me.

The courtroom had a blackened fireplace in each corner. Straight-backed chairs were aligned in rows, and along one side of the room was a platform with the judge's desk and twelve chairs for the jury. On the wall were portraits of Lincoln and Washington. A large American flag hung on one side of the room and the Missouri state flag on the other.

We passed through the courtroom, and the sheriff led us up the stairs. We went down a little hallway, and after the sheriff rapped twice on the door marked "Judge's chambers," we entered the room.

The sheriff pointed out where we were to sit. He got out his key and unlocked my handcuff from the deputy. He fastened the cuff to the chair. If I were going to run, I would have to take the chair with me. Then he fastened Ralph's cuff to his chair, and we sat down to wait for the judge. Clutter tried to cross his legs, but his chains were not long enough.

A stout man entered the room and seated himself at the table. He took his pocket watch out of his vest and, after noting the time, placed it on the table. Tilting his head down to look over his glasses, he studied Ralph, Clutter, and me. He shuffled a bunch of papers in front of him and found the one he wanted.

"John Quincy Clutter!" the judge said in a loud voice.

Clutter said, "Yes, sir." He stood up in a rattle of chains.

"You may sit down!" the judge ordered.

"Yes, sir," Clutter said. He sat back down in the chair.

The judge said, "Ralph Alonzo Collins! Also known as Poke."

"My name isn't Poke," Ralph said. His face reddened.

"Do some people call you by that name?"

"Yes, sir."

"Then you're also known as Poke!" the judge stated. Then he peered at me over his glasses.

"Warren Monroe Collins! Also known as Bob War."

"Yes, sir!" I answered.

"Well, now, Mr. Bob War. Since you are the youngest, I want you to tell me your story. I want you to tell how and when you first met Clarence Jones and Maximilian Randolph. I want you to take your time

3

and tell us everything you know about these men. Don't leave anything out. We have plenty of time."

"Yes, sir," I said. "Well, to begin with Ralph and I . . ."

"One moment!" the judge said. He motioned to a lady with a notepad. She picked up a Bible and carried it over to me. I placed my hand on the book.

"Do you swear to tell the whole truth and nothing but the truth, so help you God?"

"I do!"

"You may proceed," he said.

"Well, to begin with, Ralph always liked ghosts . . ."

CHAPTER

2

"Do you know I've never heard of one ghost in all of Tucker County?" Ralph said. "Why, there isn't even an empty house around, let alone a haunted one." He sat on the chopping block and poked the double-bitted ax into the wood chips while I gathered firewood.

I had to admit that Ralph was right.

Ralph sighed. "It just isn't fair."

"What if we dressed up like ghosts?" I asked. "Would you like that, Ralph?"

Ralph didn't say anything.

"We could dress up like ghosts and scare people like it was Halloween," I persisted.

Ralph looked at me. "I'd need to do some heavy thinking on it," he said slowly.

I knew right then and there that a ghost had been born inside Ralph's head, a dandy ghost, looking for his soul or something. I knew Ralph wouldn't rest until he had the right name and everything tied down proper.

Sure enough, that night we traipsed to Bethel Cemetery and searched all the gravestones until Ralph found a name he liked. "Peter Bottomsly," the tombstone read. "May He Rest in Peace."

"Peter Bottomsly isn't much of a name for a ghost," I said.

"But it's real, Warren," said Ralph. "Peter Bottomsly drowned at Sand Creek. Folks have to have real clues to any mystery."

We spent most of the next day out in the barn fixing up our ghost outfit. Ralph stole one of Ma's sheets. I raised Cain about him stealing the sheet, but Ralph never did listen to me. We used a wooden crate and some chicken wire, and Ralph found some red paint and black stove polish for the finishing touches. The head, molded from the chicken wire, was fastened to the box. When Ralph put the contraption on to show me, I had to admit that in the dull light of the barn, the ghost of Peter Bottomsly was real spooky.

"What's the red paint for, Ralph?" I asked.

He said it was blood.

I said, "What's so realistic about blood? Peter Bottomsly drowned."

Ralph said it was a theatrical touch.

"Ma will put a theatrical touch to our bottoms if she finds out you put red paint on her sheet."

He made me put on the ghost outfit. I slipped the crate onto my shoulders, and Ralph arranged the sheet over my head. I could tell he wasn't satisfied.

"Something is missing," he said.

He had me take the costume off. Then he fashioned a candle holder out of a tomato-can lid and nailed it to the top of the crate. He inserted a candle into the ghost's head, lit it, and tried the outfit on again.

It was darker in the barn now, and the ghost was hideous. I was sure glad I knew it was Ralph wearing the sheet. Then I had to model the costume for him. He was delighted.

"That will scare the daylights out of anyone," he said.

I got my .22 rifle and called the dogs to me, and even though the clouds were threatening rain, we gathered up Peter Bottomsly's ghost and walked down the county road to where it crossed Sand Creek at the old covered bridge.

"That's where Peter Bottomsly will appear," Ralph said. "At the scene of his death. A covered bridge isn't a haunted house, but it's the nearest thing to it."

Ralph and I had spent a lot of time playing and fishing around that old bridge. Made from oak timber and set on limestone pillars, the bridge creaked and groaned whenever a person walked over it, so you can guess what it sounded like when a wagon went across.

Horses didn't seem to mind going onto Ryan's Bridge. I guess it looked as if they were going into a barn. But, once inside, they mistrusted the creaking and groaning of the planks. The oak planks had shrunk, leaving wide spaces between the boards and exposing the giant support beams. Many of the side boards were loose, and a few were missing. We used to go out through the loose boards, balance on the side of the bridge, and jump into the water twenty feet below.

Right before the bridge, the road turned sharply and went up a steep incline. Ryan's Bridge was a perfect spot to spook a stranger because he would be inside before he could see a thing.

We sat in the darkness for a long time waiting for someone to come our way. It began to thunder and lightning, and the wind lifted and swayed the treetops back and forth. Every once in a while, a big gust of wind would rattle the loose side boards, slapping them against the beams with a loud bang. Ralph and I would jump at the sound, but neither of us would dare admit that we were scared.

The dogs had long since deserted us because of the weather, and they were on their way to the house.

Dogs are smarter than humans when it comes to weather.

Then the first jingle of harness came through the darkness. A wagon was approaching.

Excitedly, Ralph said, "Go hide at the other end of the bridge, Warren. That way you can see it all, like looking down a telescope."

As the wagon came closer, I saw Ralph strike a match and place the lighted candle inside the ghost's head. As he put the outfit on and stood facing me, I could feel my heart pound against my chest. I suddenly wished I were safe at home in bed.

The horses and the wagon appeared around the corner and came up the incline onto the dark bridge.

Ralph stood up to face the approaching wagon. "I am the ghost of Peter Bottomsly!" he shouted harshly.

The horses shied at the sight of the ghost, one backing up and the other rearing. A woman's voice cried out as the wagon started in reverse down the incline. A man's voice shouted at the panicked horses, who turned and burst into a full run back down the county road.

Ralph took off his ghost head and blew out the candle. I ran down the bridge to him. He jumped up and down, crazy with excitement.

"Ha! Did you see them? Did you hear those screams? Boy, did I scare them silly!"

We left the shelter of the bridge and stood in the rain listening to the sounds of the retreating wagon and horses.

Then the sky flared up with a long lightning bolt that crackled and flashed across the black clouds. It was as bright as day, and that's when I saw the horseman, a lone rider, coming toward us on the road. He was wearing a large hat and a rain slicker, and his horse was plodding along at a walk.

"Horseman coming," I whispered.

Ralph hurried to the middle of the bridge and knelt to light his candle. I watched from outside, peering around the support beam.

I could just see the top of the man's hat when Ralph turned and, spreading his arms, shouted in a loud voice, "I am the ghost of Peter Bottomsly!"

The horse reared, nearly throwing its rider. When the animal's front hoofs hit the ground, it started squealing and spinning around, kicking out with its hind feet. The horse's eyes glowed like embers, and steam snorted from its nostrils. Then lightning flashed, revealing the face of the rider and almost making my heart stop.

His face was like a skull with black, gaping holes for eyes. The grinning teeth opened, and a cackling laugh erupted. Pointing a bony finger, the rider spurred his horse toward Ralph, who whirled and dashed across the bridge, trying to escape. In a panic,

Ralph just banged right through the wall of the bridge. I heard him splash in the water below.

Then I realized that the horse with its wild rider was galloping right at me. I jumped over the support and dropped to the muddy ground.

The horse stomped around above me until the rider calmed it. Then the rider moved the horse to the support. He stopped. Listening! I held my breath, trying not to make a sound.

"So long, Mr. Bottomsly," the horseman shouted, and then he started laughing a harsh cackle. I trembled in the darkness beneath the bridge.

A long time passed before I ventured out from my hiding place. No one was in sight.

I traipsed up and down the creek in the rain looking for Ralph. The current had carried him in a mad rush downstream, and I found him, soaked and cold, at the sand flats. The torn sheet and crumpled-up chicken wire had caught on some hanging branches just above the water.

Ralph waded out and collected the remains, and we buried Peter Bottomsly in the sand, smoothing the grave over carefully.

As far as I know, the ghost of Peter Bottomsly stayed buried at those sand flats. Leastways, I never heard Ralph mention him again.

CHAPTER
❧ 3 ❧

I thought I had seen the last of the skeletonman. He had scared us good and proper. I thought it was over with and done for. But it wasn't. That skeletonman kept showing up and frightening us.

We were almost a quarter mile from home when our dogs commenced to bark at our approach, setting up a terrible racket. They ran to us prancing and dancing. I reckon they were a little embarrassed for deserting us. Ralph and I just ignored them.

A light appeared in the kitchen window. Either Ma or Pa was up waiting on us. They had heard the dogs barking.

We put the dogs into the barn so they would have a dry bed for the night and closed the door, locking them inside. We removed our muddy boots on the porch and set them beside the kitchen door and went inside.

Pa was seated at the kitchen table. A fire was roaring in the cookstove, and steam was blowing out of the teakettle. It was nice and warm in the kitchen.

"You boys been swimming?" Pa asked with a big grin on his face at the sight of us.

"No!" Ralph answered quickly.

"Sure, Pa," I said. "We swam all the way home."

"You look it," he said. "Get out of those wet clothes. I have some hot chocolate brewing."

Ralph and I got into some dry clothes and dried our hair while we sipped on our hot drinks.

"Where did you boys go hunting?" Pa asked.

"Down by the Garrison place," Ralph quickly lied. "We tried to wait out the storm in that old shed, but we got drenched anyway. The dogs left us when it started to rain."

As I sat there listening to the small talk and drinking my hot chocolate, I wanted very much to just blurt out what happened to us at the bridge and tell how the skeletonman scared us half to death. Pa would understand. He would probably get a big kick out of it. But Ma would skin us alive for stealing that sheet.

I figured a man might understand what we had done, but Ma would never forgive us for taking her sheet. She just could not put herself in our place. Dressing up like a ghost just wasn't her thing.

So I sat there and kept my mouth shut.

Later, when Ralph and I had gone to bed, I leaned over from my upper bunk and whispered in the darkness to him, "What are we going to do about Ma's sheet?"

"Hush!" Ralph whispered back. "We'll talk about it tomorrow."

I did not like the waiting. I would just as soon take my punishment now and not have to worry about it and dread the event.

I kept thinking about Ma's sheet and the bridge and the skeletonman until I dropped off to sleep. Then, for some reason, I was awakened and I sat upright in my bed.

There at the window was a face of a skeleton peering in at me! I didn't dare move. I just sat there frozen in the darkness of the room staring at the bony face outside the window.

The man moved his hand up to his face and pressed against the glass, trying to see into the darkness. It was the man at the bridge.

I did not even breathe, I sat so quietly. Long seconds ticked by, and the terror eased so that I could think. I tried to remember where I had left my rifle, and I tried to reason how long it would take for the man to break through the window.

Then the face was gone.

"Ralph," I whispered. "Ralph!"

Hanging onto the upper bunk I swung my arm down in the darkness trying to reach Ralph. I swung two or three times. "Ralph," I said in a low voice.

15

I dropped down from the bunk and shook Ralph awake.

"Someone was at the window!" I said.

Ralph leaped out of his bunk and stood at the empty window.

"Where?"

"There. At the window! It was that skeletonman from the bridge!"

"He must have followed us home," Ralph said.

Pa's voice boomed from the next room. "You boys hush up and go to sleep!"

"He was looking for us," I whispered to Ralph.

"No. You were dreaming, Warren. Why would the man come looking for us. He almost killed me the way it was. You were dreaming!"

"I was not dreaming. He was at the window."

The dogs began to bark in the barn. They began baying, and we could hear them scratching at the barn door.

"He's at the barn," I said.

I heard Pa's bed squeak and footfalls in the next room. Pa was going to the window. I slipped through the kitchen and into the living room to stand beside Pa in the darkness.

"Someone's out there, Pa. Someone's fooling around outside."

"You stay here," Pa said, and he took down his shotgun from above the fireplace mantel. He unbreeched the barrels and checked the load. Opening the door a crack, he peered outside and then stepped out into the darkness.

A long time passed. I heard the barn door squeak and heard the dogs dash out in a mad frenzy. They went tearing out across the field howling and baying hot on the man's trail. A person could tell where they were by the sound. They were headed for the persimmon grove north of the house. Then, the baying tone changed, they had lost the scent. After a while, Pa came back inside. He replaced the shotgun above the mantelpiece. "Go on back to bed, Warren. Whoever it was is long gone. We'll leave the dogs out."

Ralph had my rifle and was peering out our bedroom window when I returned.

"Are you sure it was the skeletonman?"

"I'm positive. He looked like a skeleton. Just skin and bone."

"What did he want?" Ralph asked, not expecting an answer.

We kept watch for a long time, just thinking about the night's events. But the dogs were quiet, so we began to feel secure again and eventually fell into an uneasy sleep.

I awoke to bright sunlight shining in the window. The aroma of coffee and bacon floated in from the kitchen. But all the pleasantry of the moment disappeared when I remembered the skeletonman at the bridge and the stolen sheet. I went from a cheerful disposition to one of despair in just an instant.

I slowly got down from my bunk and put on my clothes. I wanted to go outside to see if there were any footprints in the wet ground. Footprints would make it all real and not a dream. But Ma stopped me cold.

"Where are you going, young man?"

"Outside, Ma."

"Sit down and eat your breakfast before it gets cold."

We ate in silence, and then Pa suddenly said, "There was a man prowling around last night. From his tracks, he looked in all the windows and was going to go into the barn when the dogs cut loose and scared him away."

"Wonder what he wanted," Ralph muttered.

"Some hobo probably," Pa said. "He was looking for something to steal. I tracked him down to the persimmon grove, where he had his horse tied. He went south toward Coyville."

Ralph and I chewed on our biscuits, digesting Pa's information. I began to feel better about the skeleton-man, but I sure was worried about Ma's sheet.

"That man left the biggest footprints I have ever seen. I sure would hate to buy boots for him." Pa attempted a joke.

"Maybe that was why he was out thieving," Ma

said in a merry manner. "He needed money for a new pair of boots."

"Well, he's gone now," Pa said.

After breakfast we did our chores, and I noticed Ralph was not his usual self: he worked hard and fast. "Hurry up," he commanded. "I want to track that stranger to see where he went."

"Pa said the tracks went toward Coyville."

"Well, let's get the berries picked so we can go see," Ralph said.

We gathered our pails and picked over the blackberry patch in record time. Ma was still working at the cream pail when we came into the kitchen with the berries.

"Well, you boys must have something in mind today working so quickly," Ma said flatly. Nothing escaped her.

"We wanted to go play after we deliver the cream and berries," Ralph said.

"Well, for a little while," Ma said. "You boys be back for dinner."

CHAPTER

4

We took off down the lane toward Coyville. We took turns pulling the wagon with the berries and the pail of cream.

"We should have taken my rifle with us, Ralph," I said.

"Ma would have gotten suspicious if we took a gun."

"Yeah, I guess you're right," I said. "What are we going to do about the sheet?"

"I was thinking about telling Ma that the prowler stole it off the clothesline."

"What would a sheet be doing on a clothesline at night? And after a rain? And who steals a sheet?"

We rounded a bend in the road where clear water bubbled out from under a large slab of rock on the hill. The cold water ran next to the road and broadened out into a wide stream an inch or two deep.

From here we could see the top of the old Coyville hotel sticking up above the treetops.

We were almost to the crossing when we saw the brand-new Maxwell touring car. It had slipped into the muddy ditch. The Maxwell was black and shiny despite being mud-splattered. We hurried to it, leaving the wagon in the road, and Ralph ran his hands over the car's gleaming surface. He was almost speechless for a change. We forgot about the skeletonman.

"The engine's still hot," Ralph said. "I'll bet they haven't been stuck here very long. They probably went down to Coyville for a team to pull them out."

Ralph opened the car door and sat down behind the wheel. He was careful not to put his muddy boots inside.

"Wow," he said.

He pulled off his boots and let them drop into the mud. He played with the foot pedals and pretended to drive.

Ralph went plumb crazy around automobiles. There were only a few around town, but Ralph could always be found if one needed tinkering. He'd even persuaded the sheriff to give him a few driving lessons.

I poked my head inside. The car had the pleasant odor of new paint and leather and lilacs. The rear seat was stacked with boxes and trunks.

"I'll bet we could get this car out of the mud ourselves," Ralph said. "Think of the favor we would be
doing the owners. Why there is no telling how far
they would have to go to get a team to pull it out of
this gumbo."

"Ralph, we don't need to go fooling around with
other people's property."

"The front wheels are turned so much, it's no
wonder the driver could not back it out of here. All a
man has to do is straighten up the wheels and ease her
out."

"Ralph!" I said.

"We'll start her up."

"Ralph!"

Ralph straightened the front wheels and tried to
back the car out of the mud. The rear wheels just spun
and slung mud. He tried to go forward and then
back, rocking it. That failing, he had me push as he
raced the engine. It was no use. The car was stuck.

Ralph let the engine idle as he circled the Maxwell,
studying the situation over. Then he began looking
around the area.

"Get me some sticks and leaves and such truck,"
Ralph said. "We'll put the stuff under the wheels for
traction."

So we set to work gathering dead brush and sticks
and leaves until we had quite a pile under the car.
Ralph stomped around the rear tires.

He tried again to back the Maxwell out. But it was no use. The car was stuck bad.

Ralph went to the barbed-wire fence across the ditch and walked down to the gate. He began to un-wire the gate. He undid the barbed-wire loop that fastened the gate and removed the hedge pole of the gate.

The pole was long enough to reach from one rear wheel to the other. Ralph wired the pole to the wooden spoke of each wheel with the barbed wire strand. Giving his work a final inspection, Ralph crawled behind the wheel.

When Ralph engaged the engine, the Maxwell hopped over the pole and backward about a foot or so. The hedge pole banged against the bottom of the car. Ralph climbed out.

"It'll work," Ralph shouted. "It'll work. Unwire that side and we'll move the pole back to the other side of the wheel and do it again."

We fastened the pole to the rear wheels, and Ralph hopped the Maxwell another foot or so. It took five hops, with us moving the pole each time. Then Ralph tried it without the pole. The wheels spun slightly and caught hold of the grass. The Maxwell went shooting out backward onto the road. Ralph mighty near ran over our wagon in his excitement, but he had the car back on the road.

"I'm going to drive the car down to the crossing to

wash it," Ralph said. He took off, leaving me standing there in the middle of the road.

There was nothing to do but follow him and bring the wagon.

Ralph stopped the Maxwell in the middle of the crossing. The water was about a foot deep because of last night's rain. Ralph jumped out, stripped off his shirt, and dipped it into the water. He began to wash the car with his shirt.

I was out of breath by the time I got to the crossing. I stood watching him working like a madman as he cleaned the mud off the Maxwell.

"Ma's going to skin you alive for ruining your shirt," I said.

"I figure the man that owns this Maxwell has to be rich. He'll pay me well for getting his automobile out of the mud and for cleaning it," Ralph said. "I figure he's down at the Coyville Hotel right now waiting for someone to do his dirty work. So why don't you trot right on down there and tell him your big brother has done done it."

"Help me across the water with the wagon," I said. "We sure don't want to lose the cream and berries." Ralph sighed and reluctantly quit scrubbing. A person would have thought he was a reverend or something. He waded over to me, and between us we carried the wagon across the water.

I left Ralph shining away and pulled the wagon on

down to the store, which was the first floor of the hotel.

The Coyville Hotel was four stories high, all faded and weathered. A person could tell it had been white years ago by looking up under the eaves. The big sign proclaimed the building to be the Coyville Hotel, and on the big plate-glass window it read: Rooney's General Store.

Coyville consisted of a few houses, the hotel, two empty stores, and a church.

I carried in the berries and the cream. No one was in the store. I had to make two trips with the berries, and when I entered the second time Mr. Rooney, having heard the little bell above the door dingle, came in through the hotel door.

"I want you to run an errand for me," he said.

"Okay."

Mr. Rooney pulled me through the door and out onto the porch. He bent down and whispered his instructions to me.

"I want you to go and get John Clutter for me. You tell him that there's a city slicker here wanting to hire a hunting guide. He wants to camp out and hunt. You go tell Clutter to get cleaned up. Tell him to dress up like a big-time hunter. Clutter can earn five, maybe six, dollars a day running this dude around through the sticks. You tell Clutter that if he gets this city slicker to buy a bunch of supplies from me, I'll give him a square cut of the profits. Can you remember all that?"

"Sure," I said. "Is this man the owner of a Maxwell touring car?"

"Yeah. He said he ran off into a ditch. I was going to get Clutter to round up a team to pull him out. But there's no hurry about it. I figure the longer he's stranded here, the more he'll buy. Sara is cooking a meal for them now."

"Well, I need to talk to the man," I said.

"For land's sake, why?" Mr. Rooney asked.

"Ralph has done got the Maxwell unstuck," I said. "Ralph's shining up the car right now down at the crossing."

"Well, that changes everything. Maybe you ought to tell the stranger about his car. I'll tell Sara to slow the meal until you can get Clutter here."

"Okay," I said.

Mr. Rooney took me to the hotel dining room and opened the door. I had never been in that room before. Mr. Rooney always kept it closed.

It was a large dining room with hardwood floors and chandeliers and curtained windows. It had mostly gone to mildew and dust. Over against the wall, a table had been set with a lace tablecloth and candles. A man and a young woman, both dressed in white, were seated at the table.

A wine bottle and glasses sat beside the silverware.

27

I had never seen anyone drink wine at a table before. It must have helped their disposition because they were smiling at each other and eating lettuce and chopped carrots and mustard greens as if they were fit for a king.

Mr. Rooney said, "Excuse me, but there's a young man to see you."

I spoke up. "Are you the man who owns that new Maxwell?"

"I am," the man answered.

The man wasn't much to look at. He had a little black mustache, and he showed a lot of teeth. But the lady was the prettiest thing I'd ever seen, with the thinnest eyebrows and rosy cheeks and chalky white skin. She was a beauty.

"Well, my big brother has done got that Maxwell out of the mud for you."

"Why that's amazing," the man said. "How was he able to do it? I figured nothing but a good team of mules could get that vehicle out of the mud."

"Ralph took a hedge pole and some barbed wire and tied the pole to the wheel spokes and just jumped her out of the mud."

"What?" The man said as he chuckled.

I repeated myself.

"You said bob war," the man said.

"Yeah, Ralph used barbed wire."

"Isn't he just precious," the lady said.

"So you used barbed wire and a pole and just hopped her out of there?"

I knew he was making fun of the way I talked, so I just ignored it. He didn't talk too good himself.

"I appreciate your brother helping us with the automobile. Where is he? I would like to offer to pay him for his trouble."

"Ralph's down at the crossing washing the Maxwell," I said. "He's using his shirt to do it, too. Ma'll skin him alive when she finds out."

"I'll purchase your brother a new shirt," the man said. "I don't want him to suffer from his mother's abuse on my account."

"I'm sending Warren after John Clutter," Mr. Rooney said. "He's the hunter I was telling you about."

"Fine," the man said.

As I walked away, I heard the lady say, "Isn't the boy just a little darling!"

I wouldn't have minded having dinner with her myself.

CHAPTER

5

John Clutter was asleep in his hog-wire hammock on the front porch of his shack, and below the hammock was Carlo, a mongrel dog. Carlo yawned when I shook Clutter. I had to shake him a couple of times to get him awake.

"Clutter! Mr. Rooney wants you to take some city man hunting."

Clutter's long black hair hung down over his face. He brushed it back to stare at me. One of Clutter's eyes was crossed. I never could tell which one. I had difficulty staring him in the eye.

"Oh Lord, son," Clutter muttered. "You go tell him I'm too sick to go hunting. I haven't been feeling well at all."

"Mr. Rooney said this city man might pay as much as five or six dollars a day."

"Just to hunt?"

"That's what Mr. Rooney said."

"To hunt?"

"Yeah, he wants a guide. Mr. Rooney said for you to dress up like a big hunter, and if you get the city man to buy supplies from him, Mr. Rooney will give you a part of the profit."

"Five or six dollars! Land's sake!" Clutter still could not believe it.

"The man has a brand-new Maxwell. Ralph just got it out of a ditch."

"A rich city feller?"

"Yes."

Clutter jumped up from the hammock, awake now. He started into his house.

"What'll I wear?" he said more to himself than me.

"You had better get out of those overalls," I said. "You look like a farmer to me."

"They're all I have to wear," Clutter said. "Except there's my funeral suit."

"You're not going to a funeral."

"Well, maybe I can wear the trousers, and then I could dig up that old buckskin shirt."

"You need a hat, not that cap," I suggested.

I followed him into the little house, and Carlo and I watched as he went plowing through trunks and chests of drawers and found the buckskin shirt. The fringed shirt was old and pretty ratty. It looked like some animal had chewed a large hole around one armpit and got sick over the rest of it.

"How's this?" Clutter asked, holding up the shirt.

"Don't you have anything else?"

"Nothing but my blue work shirts and my one white one, except it's dirty."

"You better wear the buckskin shirt," I said.

"Do you think I should shave?"

"Shave and bathe," I said. "This rich man is a gentleman."

"Oh," Clutter said.

"You get cleaned up, and I'll meet you down at Rooney's."

"Okay, Ralph," Clutter said.

"I'm Warren," I corrected.

"Sure, sure, son. That's what I meant."

I reported back to Mr. Rooney and told him Clutter was getting fixed up. I collected the cream and berry money and wrapped it in my handkerchief and put it safely down in my bib pocket. I walked back out to the hotel porch to watch Ralph down at the crossing.

He was still piddling with the Maxwell, drying it now with his shirt. He walked a slow circle around the automobile, inspecting it, shining a spot here and there. Finally, he looked up toward the hotel and slowly climbed into the car. He moved it gently out of the water and drove it up to the store.

I could tell he was disappointed that I was his only

audience. He sat at the wheel in deep thought. His cap was turned backward like a racer might wear it.

The man and woman came out onto the porch. Their white clothing was bright and stiff with starch. The lady carried a black satchel. The man just beamed when he saw the Maxwell. He gave Ralph and me a big toothy smile.

"Look what a good job the boy did on the automobile," the man exclaimed to the woman.

The lady just oohed and aahed over the Maxwell's appearance.

"I'm going to give you a dollar bill for all your help," the man said.

Ralph said, "Your car could be this clean and shiny every day, if you would let me drive it for you. I know these country roads and would not be running into any mudholes."

"Are you applying for the position of chauffeur?" the man asked.

"Well, uh," Ralph stuttered, "I want to drive the car for you."

I thought Ralph was just wishing in one hand and spitting in the other, but the man studied Ralph and said, "Lucinda and I need to discuss this." He and the lady moved down the porch, where they whispered to each other and kept looking back at Ralph and me. Then they came back.

"Lucinda and I decided we need a chauffeur.

Therefore, I would like to hire you to drive for us. What do you want for wages?"

I could tell Ralph would have been willing to do it for nothing because he was in such a fever over that shiny Maxwell. But he mumbled, "Whatever you think would be a fair wage."

Mr. Rooney spoke up in a nonchalant way. "The going rate is two dollars a day for drivers," he stated.

Two dollars a day was more than my dad made!

"Fair enough," the man said. "I'll want to leave as soon as the hunter gets here and we get supplies."

"What about me!" I cried out. "Don't I get to go, too! Why should I stay home when Ralph gets to have all the fun."

"Warren," Ralph hissed through clenched teeth.

"It isn't fair," I said. I was almost in tears. I could just see Ralph getting to drive that Maxwell all over the country, hunting and fishing, and me staying at home doing his chores.

"Let's take Bob War with us," the lady said. "He can do the dishes."

"Okay, Bob War," the man said.

"I wonder if I could collect that dollar you promised me," Ralph said.

"Certainly," the man replied as he fished out the money from his jacket pocket.

Ralph headed right for the candy counter. I followed him. I knew if I was going to get any part of that money for my labor I had better speak up fast before he ate it all up in sweets.

We began to argue in front of the candies. Mr. Rooney came into the store with the strangers, and he leaned on the counter with a long list of supplies he was making for the man.

"May I pick out some candy?" Ralph asked Mr. Rooney.

Mr. Rooney frowned and waved his hand in consent. Ralph began to plunder through the candies, selecting his favorites and placing them on the counter.

"Could I bother you for a small poke for my candy?" Ralph asked.

Mr. Rooney looked up from his list. "I don't know if I have any small pokes."

"A poke!" the stranger laughed. "Did you hear that, Lucinda? He called it a poke. Why don't you just say bag or sack?"

Ralph's face turned red, and he stared down at his candy.

"Why don't you just say bag?" the stranger asked again. Ralph did not say anything.

I spoke up. "We don't use words like that in front of ladies," I said.

"What words?"

"Bag and sack," I said.

"Well, what's wrong with those words?"

"It isn't polite," I said.

"Well," the stranger began and then stopped. He turned toward the woman, who was giggling. Then he laughed. "I had better be careful about my speech in this community."

The man introduced himself as Randolph. The woman, Lucinda, was his wife. They were from Brooklyn.

John Clutter stomped through the doors, and we all turned to look at him. He was wearing an old black felt hat with a large feather stuck in the band. One of the neighbor's roosters was probably missing a tail feather.

The buckskin shirt was still wet from washing, and it covered his white Sunday shirt and black trousers. At his belt was a skinning knife Clutter used when he helped folks butcher. It was just a kitchen knife honed razor-sharp, but it was a dandy. Also in his belt was a hatchet. Just a regular old hatchet! Clutter had it there for effect, I guess. It sure didn't work for me, but maybe a stranger would be impressed.

Clutter carried his shotgun over his arm un-breeched. He always walked with his arms out as if he were carrying a pumpkin under each one. His tight boots caused him to step as if he were walking on broken glass.

All in all, he was quite something to look at. I think he cut a fine figure for the man and lady.

"I hear tell you're looking for a hunterman guide," Clutter said, and he cocked his good eye at the stranger.

"I am," Randolph said. "Mr. Rooney recommends you highly."

"I know this country like the back of my hand," Clutter said. "There ain't no man better than me when it comes to hunting."

Carlo had followed Clutter right into the store, and he headed straight for the lady. He began to sniff at her skirts and was running his nose into the creases.

I stepped over to the lady and quietly pushed the dog aside with my leg and blocked his path to her.

Carlo kept trying to nose at the lady while the men talked, and I was just as bound and determined to keep him away. There isn't anything worse than a hound dog around a well-dressed woman for embarrassing a person.

"There's squirrel and rabbit and deer and coon," Clutter was saying. "It's just whatever you're after. We can always hunt down some wampus-cat, or whiffle-birds. Why we might even find a bingbuffer or two, if you want."

"I think mountain lion would be fun," Randolph said.

"We can find you a painter," Clutter said. "We can even get us a willipus-wallipus."

"What's that?" Randolph asked.

"Why a willipus-wallipus is a . . ."

I cut in real fast because Clutter was fixing to saw off another whopper. "You're going to take Carlo with you, aren't you?"

"Why you better believe it!" Clutter said. "Carlo will tree any critter you sic him on. Why he's the best hunting dog in these here parts. I can tell what he has treed by his bark."

"What kind of dog is he?" Randolph asked.

"He's a Heinz variety Pa says," I answered.

"Is that right?" Randolph replied.

Carlo knew he was being talked about, and he responded by rolling over on his back. Then he found a flea to scratch. He sure wasn't making any impression at all. He looked like the hindquarters of bad luck.

Mr. Rooney spoke up. "I have your list of supplies all made out. We had better start loading the car if you want to make any distance today."

Mr. Rooney got the stranger and his lady off to one side to study over the supply list, and Ralph and I pulled Clutter out onto the porch. I made sure Carlo came with us.

"Don't you be lying to the stranger," Ralph said. "He ain't no mussel-head."

"That's right," I agreed. "He ain't no fool if he can afford to own that new Maxwell. He has to have some kind of brains."

"You're going to spoil everything," Ralph said, "if you keep telling whoppers."

"Well, you're right, boys. But he looks plumb crazier than a peach-orchard boar. Who ever heard of anyone wanting someone to guide them on a hunt?"

"That's the way they do it in Africa," Ralph said.

"Well, we ain't in Africa," Clutter said.

"Look, Clutter," Ralph said. "You have to go with Warren to get permission from Pa for us to go on the hunt. Don't ask Ma, ask Pa. You can convince him we need to go."

"Well," Clutter began. You could tell he didn't want to leave the store and let the stranger get away from him.

"If I don't get to drive that Maxwell for you-all, I doubt if the man will want to go on the trip. You sure can't drive," Ralph said.

"Can't he drive? Why, how did he get here?"

"Warren and I pulled him out of a mudhole this morning. Why he can't drive much at all. How far do you think you'll get on these rocky roads with him driving?"

"I'll go tell Rooney that we're running down to your place," Clutter said.

So Clutter and I headed for home with Carlo following us. I pulled the wagon, and Clutter bounced along beside me. We hurried until we got to the creek, and Clutter waded into the deep water and stood there.

"I'm soaking these boots. They're about to destroy me," he said.

We made pretty good time after that and were good and sweaty by the time we got home. Carlo heard and saw our dogs, who were running toward us. He whined and wanted to run. Clutter told him to stay. He squatted right down. Carlo was smarter than I figured. We went on, and I called our dogs to me.

Clutter talked to Pa, and I just listened. Clutter explained that he had a fool stranger paying good money to go hunting and that Ralph and I had to go along or else the deal would fall through. Clutter made it sound like a life or death situation.

Pa consented and sent me in to pack while he explained the deal to Ma. They argued pretty well for a while, and then Ma came in to help me get some things together. All in all, she took it pretty well. I sure was glad she hadn't missed that sheet yet. I didn't want to be around when that happened.

CHAPTER

6

We made good time getting back to the store. Clutter removed his boots and carried my carpetbag for me because it kept banging against my legs. I carried his shotgun and my rifle, and we just stepped out. He had me puffing to keep up with him.

He slipped on his boots at the creek after he had soaked them again. We went on up to the store.

Mr. Rooney and Ralph had been busy carrying out supplies for the trip. Stacked all around the Maxwell were boxes of groceries, some lanterns, a shovel and ax, some old tents labeled "11th Illinois Infantry," pots and pans, and a big coffeepot. I couldn't see how the Maxwell was going to hold it all.

Clutter went right to work. He told Ralph and me where to put all the items, and he got some rope and began to tie everything down. Ralph put the top down, and we piled the car full and stacked the rolled-up tents on the back of the car and tied them down. I saw right off that there wasn't going to be room for me to ride, what with the man and woman and her black satchel in the rear seat and it so crowded there that she would mighten-near sit on his lap. Clutter would be on the passenger's side and Ralph driving and Carlo riding up front.

I figured my best show was riding in back on top of the tents.

So when we got all the gear loaded, I didn't ask. I just climbed up on top of the tents and settled myself and slid my hand under the rope to hang on.

We got all settled, and Ralph started the engine. Away we went. When Ralph went to second gear, the car jerked so much that my hat flew off. I grabbed at it and lost my balance and went tumbling off the tents.

I grabbed the hat and a rope at the same time and just hung on with one hand. I was just stubborn enough not to let go of my hat. I jammed it down on my head so hard it hurt my ears. Then I reached up and got my free hand on the rope and pulled myself up onto the tents. It was a mighty steep climb, let me tell you.

I forced my feet in under the ropes real tight, and then I removed my hat and fixed the string hatband so that I could tie the hat down on my head. I didn't want to lose my balance again, and I knew Ralph wouldn't stop for money, marbles, or chalk.

I had just got my hat tied down and was relaxing a bit up there and fixing to enjoy the ride when we entered a mile section where the hedge trees grew on both sides of the road. The branches of the trees intertwined above the road. It was like being in a tunnel, and the sunlight came through the tree branches in little spotlights, frecklelike. The shadows on the road and the blurred light of the sun coming through the trees made me dizzy.

I was thinking, "What if Ralph drives under a low-hanging branch and drags me off of this car?" when a large branch about the size of a man's arm was suddenly right in my face. I threw myself backward, and it passed over me. My feet held in the ropes, but it took some muscle to pull myself upright on my perch again.

Then we were across the valley and began a long climb up the hill, which slowed us down some because the road got pretty rocky.

We made it to a big river before we stopped. The river was clear and slow moving. Clutter directed the way, and Ralph was able to head the Maxwell right in under a bluff, where we camped. The river was just a few yards away. Clutter told us what supplies to unload, and we set about fixing up the tents for the man and his wife.

It was about dark by the time we got the camp fixed. Clutter showed me how to set up the Dutch oven to roast some potatoes, and he sent Ralph down to the river to chill a bottle of wine.

We fed Randolph and Lucinda fried chicken that Rooney had prepared and baked potatoes, and there was bakery bread and jams and apple pie. It was a regular feast, and it didn't take any time to make since it was all prepared except the potatoes.

I was so excited I couldn't sleep. I should have been tired, but I wasn't. I lay there on the blanket looking up at the stars and listening to the river sounds. Off in the distance, a rain crow cooed moanfully. I sure was glad to be here on this adventure, away from the skeletonman and away from the guilt of Ma's sheet.

Clutter woke me about daybreak, and I stirred up the fire and threw a handful of coffee grounds into the coffeepot. I mixed up some biscuits the way Ma made them and poked them in the oven to bake. I broke a batch of eggs and diced up red peppers, onions, mangoes, sausage, and just a touch of garlic bulb. When Randolph and Lucinda came out of the tent, I gave them a tin of coffee and started the omelette. Lucinda bragged on the biscuits.

We all spent the day fishing. Clutter, Ralph, and I went downstream among the willows and stripped off and had a good swim and then lay out on a sandbar.

Clutter told us we were doing a good job and should do our best to keep the strangers amused and entertained. If they got bored, he said, we would be out of a good easy job.

The next day started out about the same as the first: we fished and swam, and then we did some target practicing with my rifle and Randolph's new .22 rifle. He was a poor shot. I took a couple of shots with his rifle and discovered that the sights were off. So I wedged the rifle into a fork of a small tree to hold the gun still and took a shot to see where the bullet hit and then adjusted the sight.

I fixed the rifle sights up real fine. It would hit a penny as far away as a person could see it. But it didn't matter, Randolph just couldn't shoot straight. He couldn't hit the broad side of a barn even if you turned it sideways.

Lucinda took a few shots with his rifle, and she was even worse than he was. But they were enjoying themselves. We just set up large targets for them that even a blind man could hit, and that made them feel better.

Ralph got tired of watching them throw bullets all over the countryside. It isn't any fun to shoot with someone that can't shoot. You want to shoot against someone better than you so that you do your best and learn something.

So Ralph wandered off and began to tinker with the Maxwell. He said the brakes needed adjusting and disappeared under the car for an hour or so and emerged later all greasy, but with a satisfied look on his face.

After dinner, we were all lazying around down by the river when Clutter announced that Ralph and I should go into the next village for some supplies. Ralph was eager to go. He could never sit still for long.

Clutter told me a list of things, and Randolph gave Ralph some money. Ralph and I piled into the Maxwell, and we followed the directions Clutter had given us and found the way back to the road.

The village was about two or three miles downstream, just a little sleepy place with maybe five or six stores made out of native rock. Some wagons were down by the grainery, and a Model-T was parked down by a service station, but mostly the rocky street was deserted.

We purchased our supplies and packed them in some ice we bought at the woodlot. Ralph wanted to explore, so we walked around town just looking. Ralph went into the drugstore on the corner, and I went down to the hardware store.

I was poking around the new tools, just looking, when I turned and there was the skeletonman.

My heart jumped clear up into my mouth. I couldn't breathe.

I just froze.

But the skeletonman was staring out the window. He didn't notice me. His sunken eyes peered out from the bony sockets at the bank across the street.

I tiptoed back a few steps and got a counter between me and him. Then I headed at a fast walk straight for the door. I didn't want to walk into the skeletonman's line of sight, so I ran around the building and down to the drugstore.

I pulled Ralph away from the soda fountain.

"The skeletonman is here. He is right down the street in the hardware store. I saw him."

"Did he see you?"

"No. He was busy watching the bank."

"Come on," Ralph said. "I want to see that rapscallion."

"Don't be asking for trouble, Ralph. Let's just leave. Let's just get in the Maxwell and head out of here."

"Ain't nobody scares me without paying for it," Ralph said.

He took off, heading straight for the hardware store. I had to trot to stay up with him.

The skeletonman came out of the hardware store and started across the street. He turned and glanced at us. We froze right there. But he didn't pay us no mind; he just kept walking across the street to his horse. He tossed up the stirrup and adjusted the saddle cinch as he looked up and down the street.

We ducked inside the hardware store and watched. The skeletonman monkeyed around with his horse for a while and then wandered slowly down the street.

"He ain't up to no good," Ralph said. "Come on."

We crossed over to his horse, an old roan, who was reined to a hitching post. Even though his head was hanging low, his large cow eyes darted around, watching any movement on the street, and his pin ears flicked back and forth and to the sides, listening to the sounds. He impatiently shifted his weight from one leg to another, and his tail twitched from side to side. One could tell at a glance that he was as nervous as a sinner in church and meaner than gar-broth. The horse was a regular outlaw!

"School bells!" Ralph said. "I'll fix that cooter good. I'll bust his clock and throw it over the fence. I'll defeather him plumb naked."

I told him he was stirring up trouble with a long spoon, but Ralph would not pay any mind. He had the bit clamped between his teeth and was headed for the barn.

I followed Ralph down the alley, and I complained all the way. We stopped at a calf lot, where Ralph eyeballed the tall jimsonweeds growing. Ralph climbed over the rails and gathered five large burrs from the jimsonweeds. They were still green, but plenty sharp.

Ralph placed all five burrs under the saddle while

the roan tried to sidestep away from him. One burr would have done the trick as flighty as that monster was.

We went back down the alley to watch and wait. Shortly, we saw the skeletonman backing out of the bank. He had a bag in one hand and a long-barreled revolver in the other. He shot twice into the bank and turned and ran a few steps toward the roan and then turned back and flung another round into the bank.

When he got to the roan, he slipped the reins loose with his gun hand, stabbed his toe into the stirrup, and swung his long leg over the saddle. The roan spun around as the burrs dug in, and he went to froghopping. He jumped so high that if that horse had had a feather he could have flown. He went up in the air, spun, and came down stiff-legged, bucking out and then up in the air again.

The man was trying to keep hold of the moneybag and his pistol and grab leather at the same time. Then he let go of the pistol and bag and clung to the saddle horn for dear life. About the fourth leap, the roan left the man sitting up in the air for a long second before he came down hard in the street.

I thought the man was dead for a second or two. He just lay there.

Then a shot from the bank woke him up in a hurry. The banker cut loose with a Colt pistol. I saw where the bullet hit the street, and then I heard it whine and heard the thud of it hitting a building down the street.

Plow! The banker cut loose again, and the skeletonman was on his feet, heading for the moneybag. Then plow! The banker wasted another round. The man changed his mind and headed for his pistol, which was lying in the street. He scooped it up, and both men fired at each other. Plow! Plow!

Doors began to bang open and voices shouted. The skeletonman hightailed it down the street, chasing after the roan. He looked like a windmill busted loose. The banker emptied his pistol at the scarecrow figure.

Then a barefooted man came puffing up the street carrying a shotgun.

"Robbery!" The banker shouted.

The barefooted man didn't even slow down. "Bring the car," he ordered as he hustled down the street.

"Let's get out of here," I told Ralph.

"Naw! They're going to catch him!"

"Like a dead rat, they are!" I said. "The way he was running there ain't no man alive can catch him. And suppose they do, and he sees us and lays a charge against us! What then? There ain't no need for us to be around."

We slipped on down to the Maxwell and headed

back to camp. "I sure fixed his wagon," Ralph said. "Yes, siree bob!"

"Ralph, we had better tell Clutter all about our skeletonman. What if that man comes snooping around the camp? What if he finds us? I don't want to spend my time watching shadows."

"Let me think about it," Ralph said.

From his tone of voice, I knew I couldn't argue with him. So I just let him study the situation over.

When we pulled into camp, Ralph parked the Maxwell and killed the engine. "We had best tell Clutter," he said.

We called Clutter aside, and Ralph told him the entire story: about how we had tried to scare the man at the bridge and how the man had run Ralph off the bridge and how he followed us home and peeked in the window and then about how the man robbed the bank and made his escape. Clutter just listened and bowed his head in deep thought.

"Well, this ain't no good, nohow!" Clutter said. "We had best tell Randolph and Lucinda and get them out of here. I don't think this will bust up the party. In fact, it might encourage them to go a little deeper into the hills. Then we can be ensured of a job for quite some time. Why I can take them so deep into them timbers that a coon dog couldn't find his way out without a compass."

Clutter went over to Randolph and Lucinda and squatted down beside them and began telling them Ralph's story. He did a good job, although he did stretch it a bit in a few places. I watched the couple's faces as they listened, and they were at first amused, then shocked. They questioned Ralph on what the man looked like, and Ralph told them.

"For Bob War and Poke's safety, I think we should leave right away. There isn't any need to endanger their lives," Randolph said.

So we loaded up the car in a hurry and got everything tied down secure and headed due east right into the big timber.

CHAPTER

❧ 7 ❧

We went over a trail a squirrel would have a tough time navigating. The timber was big and tall, and a person couldn't see anything for the trees. We went until it was just too dark to see. Clutter had us stop and make a quick camp. We ate a cold supper from the ice chest, and then Clutter sent us all to bed and told us not to be afraid as he and Carlo would keep watch all night.

Clutter rousted me out before daybreak to make a fire and cook breakfast. Then he and Carlo caught a quick nap. After breakfast, Clutter told Ralph to head toward the sun and promptly dozed off in the passenger's seat.

About noon we came across a dirt road, and Clutter ordered Ralph to turn south. About two miles down the road was a little village of five or six houses huddled together, and Clutter had Ralph turn east again.

We shortly ran out of road and were back in the tall timber.

That evening we parked the Maxwell in a persimmon thicket growing in a meadow. A clear stream ran nearby. It was a good site. Clutter supervised us as we made camp and gathered firewood. I fixed a big meal, and we settled down for the evening.

Clutter said that we were totally safe from the skeletonman now. We were fifteen miles from the nearest person. I believed him and slept real well that night.

The next morning Clutter was in a terrible good mood. He joked and laughed and cut up like a newborn colt. His foolishness was catching, and Ralph and I started cutting up too. And soon Randolph and Lucinda joined in.

After breakfast, Clutter announced that we were going painter hunting. Well, Ralph and I both knew that there hadn't been a mountain lion seen in our neck of the woods for years, and we doubted if there were any around here. But we didn't contradict Clutter. After all, it was his job to do the hunting, and he was just doing his job. He didn't tell Ralph how to drive or me how to cook, so we just kept quiet and allowed him to earn his wages.

We took the rifles and headed out across the meadow and into the timber. We hadn't gone but a few feet when Carlo let out a bark.

"It ain't nothing but a turtle," Clutter said. "I can tell by his bark. It's just an old turtle."

Clutter let out a strange yell to the dog, and we caught a glimpse of Carlo moving on into the timber.

Shortly, we heard Carlo barking again.

"It's just a rabbit he's trailing," Clutter informed us, and he yelled out an order to Carlo.

We went on a ways, and Carlo cut loose again barking. He had something treed. I could tell that because the barks came from the same place.

"Hey!" Clutter said. "Carlo has a painter treed! Yes, siree! Indeed he has! It's a painter, for sure!"

We got all excited and went running through the timber until we came to a little clearing with a grove of tall trees in the middle of it. Below the trees was Carlo just carrying on barking and looking up into one of the tallest ones.

Clutter stopped us and talked to us in a stern tone. "I don't want nobody hurt with this here painter now. Poke, you take Randolph's gun and stay guard here just in case he should get away. Your job is to protect Randolph and Lucinda. Bob War and I will go get that cat!"

Ralph did as Clutter told him, and as I passed him Ralph gave me a big wink. He knew it was just a squirrel, and he was getting a big kick out of playing the game.

"Aren't you going to take a gun, Mr. Clutter?" Lucinda asked.

"Why no. I don't need one. I have my hatchet," he said. "Besides ain't no one can outshoot Bob War."

I moved off a few feet from Clutter, and we walked slowly across the clearing toward the big tree.

"Move slow," Clutter said to me in a low voice. "Move like you were fixing to flush out a covey of quail."

So we stalked up to the tree real big time. Clutter went right up to the tree swinging his hatchet back and forth in a wide arc, and I stayed off to one side of the tree like a person does when he is hunting squirrel for real.

I stopped and began searching the oak for a sign of movement. Clutter walked a few feet from the tree trunk and looked up.

Just then I heard a loud snap, and I saw a yellow-brown ball drop down from above. It was four-legged and had a set of teeth and a loud squawl.

Plump! The fur ball landed right on Clutter's head, and he went over backward with a scream. The wildcat spun off his chest and headed straight toward Carlo. Carlo let out a yelp and took off in a dead run for Ralph, and the bobcat went in the other direction.

Clutter was rolled up into a ball and was kicking out with his feet and swinging his hatchet in front of his face. Strange sounds came from him. I was distracted by Clutter enough that I never squeezed the trigger even though I had the cat in my sight.

Randolph and Lucinda came running across the meadow toward us, concern written all over their faces. And way behind them was Ralph, laughing so hard that he finally fell down on the ground and rolled around.

"The cat's gone, Clutter!" I said to him harshly and in a low voice. "Hush up!"

"He cut me up good, Bob. Take a look at my face."

"Just spit on it, and get up. Be a man!"

"The cut ain't bad?"

"It ain't nothing," I said. "Why I've had blackberry briar scratches worse than that."

Clutter got to his feet. He didn't look around at Randolph and Lucinda running to him, but he knew they were there. Lucinda had her white dress pulled up over her ankles and was outrunning Randolph.

Clutter was play-acting now. He threw the hatchet into the ground disgusted. "Dadblame it all! Did you ever see the like? Slipped just as he was attacking me. Why I had him for certain."

"Are you hurt, Mr. Clutter?" Lucinda asked breathlessly.

"I'm fine!" Clutter said. "Just fine. Nothing hurt but my pride, ma'am."

"Why, you're bleeding, Mr. Clutter!"

"Ain't nothing but a scratch. Why I've cut myself worse than this shaving."

"What was that animal, Mr. Clutter?"

"Why, ma'am, don't you know?"

"Why no. It looked like a big cat of some kind."

"Was that a panther?" Randolph asked.

"Indeed, it was," Clutter said.

"I thought they were black."

"Black ones are," Clutter said. "This one was of the mountain variety."

"Your dog ran away. He was afraid of the panther." Randolph accused.

Clutter hung down his head. He didn't have an answer to the truth.

So I said, "Carlo wasn't running from the cat, Randolph. He was trying to get the cat to chase him. That way Carlo would lead the cat away from Clutter. That way both me and Ralph would have had a clear shot at him. Carlo did just what Clutter trained him to do."

"Oh!" Randolph exclaimed, enlightened now. "You have an intelligent dog, Mr. Clutter."

"Indeed I do," Clutter said. "I knew he had a panther treed."

"Why didn't you shoot at him?" Randolph said to me.

"Why," I said, "because now we're going to get that cat in a triangulation."

"What?"

"Clutter had better explain it to you," I said.

"Ain't got time," Clutter said, and he waved real big to Ralph to walk off to the right, and I hurried in a trot to the left. We went off like we knew what we were doing.

Of course, we never did see the bobcat again. We didn't expect to. And it was after dark when Carlo finally sneaked back into camp.

CHAPTER

8

The next day we went squirrel hunting. Clutter didn't try to fool the strangers about hunting some made-up weird animal. We all went hunting for squirrel, and I shot six after Carlo had treed them.

Ralph and I cleaned the squirrels, and I cooked the whole mess for dinner. Neither Randolph nor Lucinda would touch the squirrel.

I got a little upset and said we shouldn't have killed that many squirrels if they weren't going to eat them. It's a waste to kill an animal if you aren't going to use it.

Clutter pulled me off out of earshot of the strangers.

He said, "Fix them whatever they want to eat. They're strangers and don't know no better. They ain't ever eaten squirrel. They don't know our ways, so just appease them."

"Well," I said, "I reckon my mistake was in shooting the squirrels. I should have let Randolph shoot. He couldn't have hit one of them if he had shot all day."

"That's exactly what you should have done," Clutter said. "Let him have his fun."

"Well, if I had," I said, "the squirrel population would be six more in these parts."

That night at the campfire, Randolph dug out a deck of cards and wanted to play poker. Clutter declined. He protested that he just couldn't get the hang of the game. Ralph and I said we didn't know how to play, but we were willing to learn.

Randolph shuffled the cards, playing with the deck. "It takes too long to teach someone the game. A person can't learn it in one night," he said.

Pushing the cards in front of me, he said, "Take a card! Don't let me see it. Now show the card to Poke."

I let Ralph see the deuce of hearts. Then Randolph had me put the card on top of the deck. He shuffled and reshuffled and then held the deck out to where Ralph and I could see the bottom card: the two of hearts.

We selected another card, and Randolph shuffled the deck. He held the deck up to his ears as he rapidly flipped back the cards. "That card you picked is missing," he said. "Where can it be?" He pretended to search for it, and then he grabbed Clutter's hat, and there was the card in the hat.

He shuffled the cards. Then he placed a card face-down in front of me. "The three of clubs," he said. I looked at it. It was the trey. He gave me another card and called, "The nine of diamonds." It was the nine.

"How do you do that?" Ralph asked. "Are the cards marked?"

"The cards aren't marked," Randolph said. "Here, take a look, Poke."

Ralph and I examined the cards real close, but I couldn't tell one card from the other by looking at the backs of them. When we were finished, he began shuffling the cards again.

Ralph said, "If the cards aren't marked, you won't mind doing the trick with your eyes closed!"

Randolph chuckled. He closed his eyes real tight. He slowly began identifying each card as he turned it faceup. None of us could figure the trick out.

Lucinda had sat through the card tricks with folded arms. She acted very bored, as if she had seen all the tricks before.

"We didn't come all this way to play cards," she said.

"I'm just showing Bob War and Poke some tricks," Randolph muttered.

"Showing off was what you were doing!" Lucinda exclaimed.

Clutter cut in and asked if they wanted some coffee. It was just an excuse to keep them happy and to break up the argument before it got started.

Clutter kept talking. He told Randolph and Lucinda a tall yarn about a cave nearby where Jesse James and his gang buried a big batch of gold somewhere and barely escaped from the posse with their lives.

Randolph and Lucinda got all excited about the buried gold and asked Clutter how much he reckoned was buried there. Clutter said a little over a million dollars. They both wanted to leave for the Jesse James cave right away.

Ralph and I talked to Clutter after the couple were bedded down in their tent.

"Is there any truth in that Jesse James yarn you spun?" Ralph asked.

"There could be. You never know about these stories," Clutter replied.

"You're just pulling their leg, that's all. There isn't any gold."

"We could pretend there was gold," Clutter said. "We could spend two or three days hunting for it before they gave up, and we would be getting good wages for it, too."

"It ain't honest," I said. "I don't mind telling a tall

tale or two to josh them. But this is different. I don't want to play-act at hunting gold when there isn't any."

"Same with me," Ralph said. "I believe the old saying that a fool and his money is soon parted. But I'll be danged if I'll spend my time shoveling holes in the ground just to play a practical joke. The joke isn't that funny, and it sounds like the joke would be on us doing all the hard work. It's bad enough being called Poke by that city slicker."

The next day we headed for the Jesse James cave and arrived at a little bluff hanging over a stream. It was a pitiful small cave. Randolph and Lucinda explored it and poked around under the bluff. Ralph and I tried our best to act like we believed there was gold buried somewheres, but neither one of us volunteered to get the shovel from the car.

After we had walked the length of the bluff, Randolph asked me point-blank if I thought there was any gold around.

I didn't feel like telling a fib, so I said I didn't reckon there was.

I guess that cut it, because pretty soon Randolph said that we would have dinner and then continue our trip. He wanted Clutter to find us a town big enough to have a hotel. He said he wanted a hot bath and a soft bed for a change.

It was a pretty good town that Clutter found for

them. It was nestled down in a long valley. As we came down the grade to the town, we saw a carnival on the outskirts. Ralph and I eyeballed it pretty good as we drove by, and I had my heart set on a Ferris wheel ride and cotton candy.

We got Randolph and Lucinda settled into the hotel, and Clutter collected our wages. We left in the Maxwell, and Clutter directed Ralph to drive to the outskirts of the town again. About a quarter mile from the carnival, Clutter had Ralph turn into a lane that went to a farmhouse. Clutter went up to the house and talked to the farmer for a long time. He returned and had Ralph park the Maxwell in the farmer's barn.

"I rented the barn for the night," Clutter said. "This way the car will be safe, and we can sleep in the hay and not have to pitch tents. We'll be free to go to the carnival."

Ralph was pleased. Old Clutter knew his ropes. He wasn't born yesterday.

"Do you want to cook supper for us, Bob War, or do you want to buy some hot dogs with relish and mustard at the carnival?" Clutter joked.

I said he didn't have to ask. Clutter divided up our money and gave Ralph and me our pay. I held back a few dollars and stowed the rest of my cash in the butt of my rifle. Then I buried it in the hay manger. I figured if someone stole the Maxwell at least they wouldn't get my rifle and cash money.

We hoofed it on over to the carnival, and it was getting dark by that time. But the bright lights made it just like daytime. Ralph and I had us a ball. We stuffed ourselves with hot dogs and root beer and cotton candy.

We looked over some of the games offered and watched a man try to pitch a ball into a basket and make it stay inside. No matter how hard or soft or at what angle he tossed it, the ball would just bounce out.

The man who sold the chances asked me in a loud voice if I wanted to try to make the ball stay inside the basket. I said I reckon not, for if that man couldn't make one stay inside with as many tries as he had, then I reckon I would turn down a chance for myself.

We moved on down a ways to a booth that had .22 rifles chained to the counter, and there were little targets maybe ten feet away with black dots. Big teddy bears hung all around the targets.

"Why don't you try your luck at the rifles, Bob War," Clutter said. "You might win us a teddy bear."

"I don't want no teddy bear," I said.

"Come on, boys," the man at the counter said. "Three shots for a dime!"

"What do you win?"

"That big teddy bear," he said.

"What would I do with a teddy bear?" I asked.

"Give it to your sweetheart."

"I don't have a sweetheart."

"Then give it to your mother!"

"Ma don't want a teddy bear."

"Are you going to shoot or what?"

"I ain't going to shoot for no teddy bear," I said.

"What about you, mister?" the man asked Clutter.

"Bob War is the shooter," Clutter said. "Myself, I ain't interested. I have to use a shotgun to hit anything."

"Tell you what, kid. If you can cut out all of the black dot, I'll give you a dollar."

"Sounds good to me," I said. "Except nobody can cut out that black dot with three shots no matter how well a body clustered his hits. You allow me six shots at the black dot, and I'll erase it for you if these sights are true."

"There ain't nothing wrong with the rifle, boy. I tell you what I'll do. You pay me one dollar for six bullets, and I'll give you a ten-spot if you can cut all the black off a dot."

"Done!" I said. I plunked down a dollar, and the man grabbed it up, and then he put six shells into the rifle.

I pulled down on the dot and marched a tight pattern right around the dot. I cut out the dot in five shots.

"Give me my ten dollars," I said.

"Look, kid, don't you want the teddy bear?"

"I want my ten," I said. "I did it with five shots, and I still have one left in the barrel."

He tossed down a crumpled ten-spot. "Go on and get out of here," he said.

We went on down and fished for a prize, and we tossed rings into some bottles but we didn't win anything, so we quit.

We passed a big painted tent with a lot of weird pictures. The man was yelling out what all we would see if we paid twenty-five cents to get inside. We got our tickets and went into the tent and stood there near a platform for a while. Pretty soon a woman came out in skimpy underclothes and showed us her tattoos. She had them all over her body. There wasn't a spot I could see that wasn't colored. She wasn't much to look at.

Then a man came out and ate fire. I didn't think much of it. But the sword swallower was something else. Then there was a man who sewed his mouth shut with a real needle and thread. And a little lady who had this big snake about ten foot long. Well, it was all interesting enough, I guess, for a quarter.

We came out of the tent, and Ralph and I were

headed for the Ferris wheel. Clutter had wandered off somewhere, and we were just standing there waiting and looking for him. We were next to the merry-go-round, and the wooden horses and giraffes and lions were going around and around, and the music was so cheerful.

Then we saw the skeletonman. He was leaned up against the unicorn, just staring out over the crowd. There was a deadness in his eyes like he was all by himself and he was just looking for a pesky fly that was bothering him.

Ralph and I saw the skeletonman at the same time. I froze in my tracks, and I heard Ralph gasp. Ralph pulled me behind the nearest tent before the unicorn appeared again.

We peeked from behind the tent, and as the merry-go-round came round the skeletonman looked right at us, and he held his gaze on us as the merry-go-round turned.

Ralph said, "He's seen us. He knows us, Warren. Let's make some tracks!"

We took off at a run, looking for Clutter. I glanced back at the merry-go-round, and the unicorn was empty.

"He's coming after us for sure," I said.

We pushed through the crowd, and there we saw Clutter's black hat above the people gathered around a barker. We pushed into the mass and grabbed hold of Clutter.

"Let's go, Clutter," Ralph said in an anxious voice, and Clutter didn't ask any questions, he just broke into a run with us. We got away from the carnival fast.

We made the farmer's barn in a dead run. Clutter swung open the barn doors, and I dug out my rifle from under the hay and slid a shell into the chamber. Clutter unbreeched his shotgun and loaded her up. We climbed in the Maxwell and headed out for town.

Ralph stopped in front of the hotel, and from my perch aboard the rolled-up tents, I could see through the big plate-glass windows into the hotel dining room. Randolph and Lucinda were dressed in splendid pastels, dining at a candlelit table.

"They're eating inside," I yelled to Clutter.

Clutter busted through the doors and went right to the table. I don't know what he said, but Lucinda's hand went up to her mouth, and she just flew out of the dining room. Randolph tossed some money on the table and then went over to the register desk. Clutter came outside and stood in the hotel doorway with his shotgun.

Lucinda came down the stairs with a suitcase in each hand and her black satchel tucked next to her body. Randolph took the bags from her, and they all hurried to the car. Ralph took off the second they were seated. Nobody said a word. Clutter kept watching ahead, and I twisted around and watched our rear.

We got out of town fast and had a good dirt road ahead of us. Everyone relaxed after a mile or two. We drove all through the night. A body can't get much sleep perched up on top on the baggage. I roped my legs down good, so if I did doze off I wouldn't fall. I had time to do a lot of thinking.

"Why were Randolph and Lucinda so frightened by the skeletonman," I thought to myself. "They haven't done him any harm." And then when Randolph got into the car I noticed a big pistol under his jacket. I had never noticed it before. And he had had it on him at the table. And Lucinda sure clung to her black satchel. I thought about it all for a long time.

CHAPTER

9

We drove all that night, and Ralph slept for a few hours the next day after lunch, and then we were on the road again. About the third day the hills got higher and the valleys deeper. It was slow going.

On the fourth day, we crossed into Arkansas, and we stopped at a little town above White River. A lot of people milled around the streets. Trucks and mule teams hauled timber to a sawmill on the side of the hills, and smoke hung over the valley from the charcoal mills.

"This is a good place to stop for the day," Randolph said.

We parked beside a group of little log cabins, and Randolph went into the office and rented a couple of them.

Ralph and I carried all their luggage into their cabin while Clutter supervised. Then Clutter asked for our wages, and Randolph counted out our money into Clutter's hand.

"I got to get some gravel for my goose," Clutter said to Randolph.

"What?" Randolph asked.

"Got to wet my whistle."

"Oh."

Clutter, Ralph, and I had a cabin next to Randolph and Lucinda's. Ralph and I moved everything into the cabin, and we got settled. Clutter was restless. I figured the money was burning a hole in his pocket. He counted out our wages, and we waited around for Lucinda and Randolph.

We all walked up to the Red Onion Inn for supper. The inn, a two-story structure of unfinished lumber, filled a large hole of sheer rock made where the mountain had been blasted to make room for the building.

The inside of the inn smelled of smoke, beer, and heavy perfume. A mess of people were seated at dining tables, and a bar ran the length of the room in front of a long mirror. In the next room were easy chairs and sofas, and the center of the room was bare for dancing. On a raised platform in the corner of the room, a band of four men was sawing away at a waltz.

We seated ourselves at one of the tables, and Randolph ordered steak for us. Randolph left the table and went down to the bartender and struck up a con-

versation with him. Clutter and Ralph went off to
talk to a large lady seated in the doorway.

Lucinda and I watched the couples dancing in the
next room.

"This is a nice place," I said to Lucinda. "Would
you like to dance?"

"No," she said. "I don't want to dance here."

So I excused myself from the table.

I saw a girl maybe sixteen or seventeen seated beside the dance floor. I went over and asked her if she
would like to dance. She smiled at me as if it would
be a big joke to dance, but she rose and I led her out
on the dance floor. The music was loud, a little
twangy, but middling good, and the tune was beauti-
ful to waltz after.

The girl worked at the inn she said. She was a good
dancer and allowed me to lead. She didn't try to push
me around because I was younger or shorter. She was
a nice girl.

We finished the waltz, and the band struck up a
two-step, and we danced to that number. We were
starting our third dance when a big man stopped us.
He took hold of the girl's arm.

"I need to borrow your sweetheart for a while," the
man said to me.

The girl smiled at me.

"Thank you for the dance," she said. "I have to go
to work."

"Thank you," I said.

The girl led the man upstairs. As I went back to the table, I saw that our food had arrived and Ralph and Clutter were missing. I ate my meal. Randolph and Lucinda began arguing as they ate. He had evidently found a poker game in the back room.

"They're just hayseeds back there with plenty of green. I'll make a killing."

"That's what you always say."

"I'll just take a few hundred," he said.

"Well, you'll not take my share, that's for certain! And what am I expected to do while you're in there gambling?"

"Enjoy the atmosphere," he said.

I sidled up to the band platform, looking over the girls and getting ready to make my choice for the next dance when the band came to the end of its number.

The banjo player spoke to me.

"Hey, kid. You're a pretty good dancer," he said. "Can you dance a jig?"

"Well, I clog a little," I said.

"Let's see what you can do."

The band struck up "The Irish Washerwoman." It didn't bother me any to dance by myself. We did it all the time back home. So I stepped real lively to the music and tapped out the rhythm.

When they finished that tune, they swung right into another and didn't allow me a chance to rest. I danced to the music while all the people sat watching me.

"Let's take a break, boys," the banjo player said, and the players put down their instruments and wandered off the platform toward the bar. The banjo player hung back.

Some of the men in the room came up, and they poked some money into a fruit jar beside the platform. "You're a good dancer," one of the men said. They all told the banjo player how much they enjoyed the music.

"Where you from, boy?" the banjo player asked me, and we struck up a conversation.

His name was Reuben Mars, but everyone called him Freck. I told him I was called Bob War, but my real name was Warren Collins. Freck wanted to know if I would dance some more for the band.

"Sure," I said. "I'll dance for you until Clutter and Ralph get ready to leave. I don't know where they went to."

"Well, Bob War, they're probably upstairs getting their bells rung."

"What?"

"They're probably talking to some of the people."

"Yeah," I said.

Freck offered me a permanent job dancing for the band. I told him that we were just passing through.

He pulled a dollar bill out from the fruit jar, and he

said that was my wages for dancing. The dollar was mine if I danced until my partners returned.

I put the money in my pocket, and I seated myself at the table. Lucinda was staring off into space.

"I'm going back to the cabin," she said. "If Randolph wants me, that's where I'll be."

I could tell she was worried about Randolph.

I said, "Randolph can take care of himself. The way he handles cards, he won't lose."

"That's what I'm afraid of!"

"What do you mean?"

"If they catch him doing any tricks, he'll be in bad trouble," she explained.

I walked her down to her cabin and returned to the inn. Shortly, the band got together again and started another jig number. I went back to work.

I danced about five tunes out, and some of the people clapped their hands at the end of each number.

Clutter came downstairs first, and a little later Ralph came down. They seated themselves at the table and started eating their cold meal. I joined them at the table just as Randolph came out of the back room.

"Where's Lucinda?" Randolph asked. I could tell by his mood that he had lost his money.

"Lucinda is down at the cabin," I said.

Randolph left us without a word.

"You about ready to shove off?" Clutter asked.

"Whenever," I said.

Clutter and Ralph finished their food, and we got up to leave. I waved at Freck and his band. I followed Clutter and Ralph out of the inn.

"That sure was a nice place," I said. "We'll have to come back again."

"We will," Clutter said.

CHAPTER

❦ 10 ❧

We passed Randolph as we walked back to the cabin. He was headed back to the card game.

"Good luck," Clutter said to him as we passed, but Randolph didn't answer.

"I sure wouldn't ever gamble with him," Ralph said. "He does too many card tricks too easy. That just might give him the tendency to cheat a mite."

"Do you think he would cheat at cards?" I asked.

"Well, he had to get all his money somehow," Ralph said. "I sure can't picture him working. Can you?"

"I never thought about it."

We slept in the next morning. I woke up at daybreak but remembered that I didn't have to cook breakfast, and I drifted back to sleep. Ralph and Clutter woke me up later. We went outside the cabin and stood around killing time because Clutter felt obligated to wait until Lucinda and Randolph were up for breakfast.

"They know the way to the Red Onion Inn," Ralph said. "We ain't going to serve them breakfast in bed."

Clutter said, "Maybe we ought to awaken them."

"Go ahead," Ralph said. "Warren and I are going to eat."

Lucinda came out of her cabin and joined us.

"Good morning, ma'am. Where's Randolph?" Clutter asked very politely.

"Down at the inn gambling," Lucinda said. "He hasn't been back to the cabin."

The inn was pretty quiet and mighty near empty except for a couple of lumbermen eating at the corner table. We seated ourselves, and the cook came over to take our order.

"Is that card game still going on in the back room?" Lucinda asked the cook.

"I don't know anything about any card game," the man said.

"Well, go take a look!" Lucinda shouted. "My husband is back there playing cards."

"Oh! Well, yes, the game's still being played," the cook said. "They ain't left yet."

We were almost finished with our breakfast, when Randolph came out of the back room. He came to our table, and Lucinda lit right into him. He was all red-eyed and had his shirt unbuttoned and his tie loose. He looked like he had been rode hard and put away wet.

Lucinda did not stop for air: "Well? Are you satisfied now? A bunch of hayseeds, you said. A bunch of hicks! How much did you win? Where's our money now? Lining the pockets of those clods?"

"They kept calling for a new deck every few minutes, and they had a dealer!"

"Oh my! You mean those dumb hicks were intelligent enough to bring in a cold deck before you could mark them? Oh my! My!" Lucinda rattled on. "And their own dealer! Well, my goodness! Randy couldn't stack the deck?"

"Lay off," Randolph said, red-faced.

"You bet I'll lay off!" she screamed. "Why did you play cards with them if you couldn't manipulate the deck!"

"They're a bunch of clods!"

"But they have our money!"

Clutter motioned to Ralph and me, and we moved away from the table and left the inn. She was still giving him the what-for when we left. I felt sorry for the man.

As we walked back to the cabin, Clutter said, "We got to do something, boys. It's bad. Real bad, them fighting. We have to keep them entertained or else we just might be out of a job."

"I think they're tired of hunting and fishing," Ralph said.

"And Lucinda won't dance," I said.

"Well, I'll ask around and see if there isn't something that might amuse them," Clutter said.

When Randolph and Lucinda joined us, you could tell Randolph had had his comb wilted. He had his tail between his legs and a real sour look on his face.

"Maybe you would like to go out to the stockyards," Clutter said. "Some of the local folks are practicing for a rodeo that's coming to town. They're practicing calf roping and bull riding and bronco riding."

"It might be interesting," Randolph said.

Clutter spoke in a low voice so that Lucinda didn't hear. "And some of the boys make some side bets on the events."

"Quite a lot of betting?"

"It gets pretty heavy at times," Clutter replied. "They will bet on anything."

Randolph's face changed, and he perked up. He was ready to go right then. But he had to talk Lucinda into going, so he pulled her to one side. We let them haggle in private.

We stopped on the rise overlooking the stockyards, which were nestled in a little valley. Randolph had Ralph stop the Maxwell. A rail fence surrounded the holding corral and rail gates connected the corral to the rodeo area, where split-rail seats had been set up. Maybe twenty cowboys were milling around the arena.

"Poke, can you fix this car up so that it sounds terrible? Maybe you can cross a couple of spark-plug wires?" Randolph asked Ralph.

"Why would you want to do that?" Ralph asked.

"I just want to play a little joke," Randolph said in a cheerful voice. "Just a little trick on the locals. Come on, Poke, humor me."

Clutter nudged Ralph. Ralph opened up the hood and tinkered with the engine. He closed the hood and got back into the car and started the engine. The entire car shook as the engine idled.

"Can you make it backfire as we drive up to the men?" Randolph asked.

"Whatever you say," Ralph said.

We headed across the pastureland toward the arena.

"Don't drive into any of the cow manure, Poke," Randolph shouted. "I don't want the car messed up."

Ralph dodged a cow pile and swerved to miss another.

"There's one," Randolph shouted. "There's one, Poke! There's another! Swing out! Miss it!"

Ralph was driving like a drunken sailor on leave, weaving from one side to another. The Maxwell sounded like the broken running gears of a grasshopper, backfiring and chattering. We came to a stop in front of the cowboys, who were grinning and laughing at Ralph's driving.

I could see the back of Ralph's neck getting beet-red. He was mortified to be caught driving an automobile sounding like this one. He killed the engine and just sat there like a statue.

Randolph stepped out of the car and didn't stop talking for one second. I never heard a man talk so much and so fast at one time. Before we could get out of the car, Randolph had handed them a line of talk about what a fast car the Maxwell was. He was wanting to find someone with an automobile to race.

A short wiry cowboy seated on the top rail pushed back his Stetson and said, "Why I got me a little cow pony that can outrun that thing."

"There isn't a horse alive that can outrun this car," Randolph said.

"Well, I got a few coins that says my pony right over there can," the cowboy said.

"How much money do you want to wager?" Randolph asked, and he pulled out a handful of bills.

"Well, now. Let's talk about the racetrack first. I'll bet you my pony can outrun that there car around this corral. Once around the corral or twice if you want," the cowboy said.

"Done!" Randolph agreed. "Two times around the track. Put up your money!"

"One more thing," the cowboy said. "I don't want my pony run over by no car. So you run your car on the inside of the corral or the outside, I don't care. But me and my pony want a fence between us and that there automobile."

"The one who takes the inside of the corral has the shorter distance!" Randolph said.

The cowboy shrugged with a smile.

"We'll take the inside track then," Randolph said. "But first we need to let my driver tune the engine."

"That's just fine and dandy," the cowboy said as he pulled some money out of his pocket. "Who's going to hold the bets?" he asked.

One of the men said, "Let the kid hold the bets."

"I agree," Randolph said. "Bob War can be the banker."

The men began poking money into my hands, and Randolph slowly counted out money to cover the bets.

One of the men tapped me on the shoulder, and I looked up at him. It was Freck from the Red Onion Inn.

"What do you think, Bob War?" Freck asked me. "Do you think that Maxwell can outrun Billy's pony?"

Randolph was busy talking to the men and couldn't hear me, so I said, "Put a dollar in the pot for me, Freck."

Freck grinned, and he poked Randolph to get his attention. "Eleven dollars for me."

Ralph set to work on the engine, and the men didn't move from their places. But one of them, I don't know which, yelled out, "You had best uncross them spark-plug wires, boy!" They all laughed.

A couple of the cowboys rounded up the horses in the corral and headed them into the arena. Then they opened up the rail gate to the corral and took down the rails connecting the arena and loading pens.

Ralph started the engine and drove the Maxwell up to the corral gate. Only then did Billy climb down from the fence and saunter over to his pony and mount. He sat astride him real easy, just like he was a part of the horse. The smile never left his face for an instant, even though the pony pranced and darted and tried to rear up. Billy just cooed to the pony to calm him.

"The race commences when I fire this shotgun," a man said to Billy, and Billy nodded. The man stepped over to Ralph and told him the same thing.

Billy's horse shied, and Billy circled him around and finally sidestepped him up to his starting position on the outside of the corral.

I don't know if it was the shotgun blast or Billy's

spurs, but at the sound of the gun that pony just squatted and leaped about thirty feet into a dead run. He was quick.

Ralph never stood a chance. He didn't even get the Maxwell out of second gear until after the second turn. The pony just hugged the rail fence and ran flat out like a house afire. He made a complete circuit of the corral by the time Ralph had gone three-quarters. Ralph did his best, but it wasn't any use. The tight little track didn't work to the advantage of an automobile.

The pony flashed by the finish line and spun back in a tight circle like he was weeding out a steer. Billy stepped down from the saddle with the big smile still on his face. He came over and took the money out of my hand.

"Want to go two out of three?" Billy asked Randolph. All the men laughed and collected their money. Freck sidled up and crammed my winnings into my pocket.

I took a glance over at Lucinda, and I could tell she was fit to be tied. I figured Randolph would sure catch Billy Ned when she got him off by himself. She walked over to the automobile and, head held high, seated herself in the backseat and opened her parasol.

Randolph took the teasing real well; he didn't hang his head or anything, but smiled real pleasant like losing money didn't mean a thing to him. The men razzed him pretty good: one wanted to go get his grandmother to run against the Maxwell. He said she would run barefooted. The men laughed at that.

Randolph said, "I was told you boys will gamble on anything. How about a shooting contest? Double or nothing!"

"You going to be doing the shooting?"

"No, the boy here, Bob War," Randolph answered.

They were quiet all of a sudden. Then, "Where you from, boy?" one of the men asked me.

I told them.

"Well, I reckon he knows how to shoot then," another man said.

"What do you think, Oscar?" Billy asked a potbellied man with wire spectacles. "Do you want to shoot against Bob War?"

"I don't have my rifle," Oscar answered.

"Use mine!" Randolph said as he removed his .22 from the Maxwell. "It's a new one."

Oscar handled the gun, feeling the weight. He put it to his shoulder and sighted down the barrel.

"Got a shell?" he asked.

Randolph opened a box of .22 cartridges, and Oscar took one and inserted it into the chamber. He drew a bead on a fence post about sixty feet away and squeezed the trigger.

"Nope," Oscar said as he handed the rifle back to

Randolph. "The sights aren't quite true, and I don't feel like playing any shooting games using Kentucky windage."

"What do you mean the sights are wrong? It's a new rifle. I just bought it a few days ago!" Randolph protested.

Oscar shrugged. "Well, whatever you say, mister. But I ain't shooting that weapon for any bet. I'm dry behind the ears!" Oscar leaned into the Maxwell and picked up my rifle.

"Hey!" I said. "That's my gun."

"Sorry," Oscar said. "May I look at it?"

"Sure," I said. "It's okay. Go ahead and shoot it if you want."

The stock was too short for Oscar, but he fondled it and brought it up to his shoulders and sighted down the barrel. He extracted a shell from the box and inserted it into the chamber and locked it. Then, cocking back the hammer, he sighted down the barrel again at the same post. He squeezed off the round.

"This is a good rifle," he said. "We'll shoot with the kid's gun."

One of the men dug an empty Prince Albert can out of a trash barrel, and Oscar carried the can out about a hundred paces and set it on the ground as a target.

Oscar returned to us and announced: "One shot for each of us. Whoever gets nearest to the flower on

Prince Albert's coat wins. We flip a coin to see who shoots first."

"How much money do you want to bet?" Billy asked Randolph.

"I'll cover all bets," Randolph said in a loud voice.

The cowboys dug out wadded-up bills from their pockets and pressed around Randolph to make their bets. When they were finished, Oscar said, "Someone flip a coin."

I lost. So I shot first.

I held the rifle against a fence post to steady it and lined the can up in my sights. At that distance, you can't actually see the carnation on Prince Albert's lapel, but you know where it is on the can. I gently squeezed the trigger.

The can rocked easy, and I knew I had made a good hit. Billy and Randolph walked over to the can to see where I had hit it.

"About a half inch from the flower," Billy said in a loud voice.

The two men stood back from the can, as Oscar placed the gun barrel of my rifle on top of the post to steady it. He inserted the shell and locked the chamber. He cocked the hammer and squeezed the trigger.

The can flinched from the bullet. Billy picked up the can and waved it.

"A quarter inch off," he said. "Oscar is the closest."

The men collected their bets and passed the can around, examining the bullet holes. They all patted Oscar on the back and were in a good mood.

Ralph had been real quiet and had been standing around with his hands tucked in his pockets. He'd been shamed when he lost the race, and now that his brother had lost the shooting match, he couldn't keep quiet any longer. He had his pride to think of.

"Anybody can hit a can at that distance," he said in a big voice. "Why don't we set up a real target that takes skill?"

The cowboys were silenced by his outburst, although some of them grinned and winked at one another.

Ralph picked up an empty peach can, and he peeled back the paper from the shiny tin. He walked out across the pastureland and placed the can against an old stump. It was a long ways off.

When Ralph returned to us, he dug out all his money from his pocket and counted it. "I've got seven dollars and sixty-five cents that says my little brother can hit the can from here."

Billy asked Oscar, "Do you want to shoot the can, Oscar?"

"By dogs, Billy, I can barely see it at this distance."

"That's a real target, mister," Ralph taunted. "Why, I might be able to hit it myself. Of course, I ain't as good a shot as my brother, but I wouldn't be afraid to try."

"The kid is calling your hand, Oscar," Billy laughed. The cowboys began chiding Oscar until he nodded his head in consent.

Clutter put up all the money he had, about three dollars, and I emptied my pockets. When Freck saw me betting, he yelled out that he was betting on Bob War.

Randolph said, "Gentlemen, you have broken me completely, but if my IOU is any good I would like to cover all bets. I'll cover the bet with the Maxwell."

That took the men back for a second or two, but most of them bet all their money. All except Billy.

"I think I'll go with the kid, boys!" Billy said. "I do believe we are playing his game now!"

The men got pretty quiet when we got ready to shoot. Billy and another man walked out to the target so they could see the bullets hit.

"I go first," Oscar said. He lined up the target in his sights and took a long time before he fired.

Billy waved his hand. It was a complete miss.

Now it was my turn. I took my rifle, inserted the shell, and lined up the can in the rifle sights. I took a deep breath, tried not to think of anything but that can, and touched off the trigger.

The can jumped up high, and I knew I had just nicked it. But I had hit it.

Some of the men groaned when they saw the can jump. Oscar was the first to pat me on the back, and most all the cowboys said it was a good shot.

We collected our money, and I was feeling real fine. One of the cowboys said, "That's the best shot I've ever seen. Do you think you could do it again?"

"Sure," I said, real cocksure. "How much do you want to bet?"

"I'm flat busted, kid. Your pals have got all my money. I just want to see you do it again so as I know I didn't lose my wages on a fluke shot."

"Okay," I said. "I'll shoot again and prove it to you."

I put a shell in the chamber and was locking the chamber when Billy said, "Don't be shooting for free, boy. Make them pay to play your game. I'll bet Bob War can hit the can again."

There weren't any takers.

I lined up the target and made the can jump again. "Well, as I live and breathe," one of the men said.

Ralph held his head real high when we left. He was as proud as a peacock with two tails. Randolph was right-down pleasant too, since he had more money than he started out with. Even Lucinda was smiling.

Back in town Clutter struck up a line of talk with the local whittlers out in front of the general store and swung the subject around to Eureka Springs. The old-sters didn't think much of the town, but the two younger ones bragged it up big. They told a story about a hotel being thirteen stories high, and yet on the thirteenth floor you could walk out onto land because the hotel was built on a steep mountainside.

Ralph and I just listened to the talk and the bragging about Eureka Springs, but we made a note in our heads to remember things so that we could help Clutter convince the outlanders to journey on to Eureka.

It really didn't take much to convince them. Clutter began telling them about the fancy hotels and the social clubs and about how all the rich people came there to bathe in the magic waters to cure their ailments. They were sold real quick and were ready to start. Clutter didn't even get a chance to finish his spiel.

Randolph rented the cabins for a few more nights to store all our tents and hunting equipment, and he hired a man to take care of Carlo. He even had Clutter and me store our guns, and Clutter left his hatchet and skinning knife.

The Maxwell was empty now except for our luggage. I rode up front with Ralph and Clutter. I even got to sit in Carlo's place.

CHAPTER

11

I'd never seen a town like Eureka Springs, before nor since. The town was spread over two or three mountains, and the houses were all clinging to the mountainsides. Each house had wooden steps going up to it, or stone ones. One house was five stories high counting the gables, and it had five chimneys. The steps going up to it zigged and zagged so that it wouldn't be so steep walking. The man that owned that house probably drove around up the back side of the mountain and came in his backdoor, where it was level, and made folks that came visiting climb those steps.

The streets were paved, and on each side was a limestone wall built so that the mountain didn't cave in. Little parks built around springs were at every turn. In each park stood a little house that could be used as a bandstand or just as a place where a person could rest after getting a drink of water. Most of the parks were at street level, although I saw one or two you had to climb a bunch of steps to get to.

The town had a lot of stores and businesses and suchlike. There were a lot of hotels and even an opera house. The streets were just filled with ladies and gentlemen milling around in all sorts of silks and satins and jewels. Somebody said that the people came here for their health, to drink and to bathe in the healing waters. I reckon the water must have done some good because everybody sure looked healthy to me.

Randolph had us drive around the town until we had seen it all. Then he had Ralph take us to a hotel downtown. Randolph went in with Clutter and me and registered us. Clutter and I stayed in the lobby while Ralph drove Randolph and Lucinda up to the mountaintop to the Crescent Hotel, which looked like a castle, all tall and made of limestone. It was a monstrous big building, and fancy, too.

When Ralph returned with the Maxwell I could tell he was ticked off about something. His lower lip pouched out. I asked him what was troubling him.

"Oh, that Randolph! Treated me like I was a servant! He said, 'Poke, go service the Maxwell and check in on me about one o'clock tomorrow'!"

"So what did you say?"

"I said, 'Yes, sir.' It wasn't what I wanted to say, but I know what side my bread is buttered on."

Clutter said, "Well, them kind are used to servants, I reckon. We just got to go along with them."

"I know," Ralph said. "But it's pretty tough play-acting sometimes."

Ralph cheered up when he saw the hotel room. There were two brass beds, a big table and chairs, and some soft easy chairs. One door led to a big closet, and another door led to a big bathroom with a large porcelain tub, a sink, and a toilet.

Ralph got excited about the toilet. He opened it up and looked at it and pulled the chain to flush it. He watched the water run.

I had to help him move in a table so he could climb up on it to get to the flush box. Ralph was curious about how the toilet worked. He had to stand on a chair on top of the table in order to see the water fill. He would flush the toilet and wait for it to fill and then flush it again.

"So that's how it works," he said.

Clutter taught Ralph and me how to play pool in the downstairs room of the hotel. After a few games, we had dinner at the hotel and charged the meal to Randolph. Then we explored the town. We took a drink at every spring. It was good water well enough. But I doubted if there was anything magic about it. Leastways, I didn't feel any different for drinking it.

We saw this church that was built against the

mountainside. It was made of limestone with a red-tiled roof. A person had to enter through the archways of the bell tower and go down stairs to get into the church. There wasn't any other entrance. But we didn't go inside, because Clutter said it was a Catholic church and you had to be a Catholic to enter.

By the next day, we were all broke. It didn't take long for us to spend our money. I had purchased two cotton sheets for Ma to replace the one Ralph and I had stolen. Then I got to thinking about giving Ma those two sheets, which would be an admission of guilt, so I went back and bought two more sheets so I could give her four as a gift. I wrapped the sheets in some nice brown paper and tied it up good with twine.

I felt much better than I had in days after I got those sheets, but Ralph and Clutter were in a stew with no money to spend. Clutter told Ralph to collect our wages from Randolph when he went to see him at one o'clock.

Ralph went up on schedule and soon returned empty-handed. Randolph and Lucinda were out on a sightseeing tour with a group, Ralph was told. So we hung around town watching the people walk by. We didn't have any money, but we had a good room and good food. Anything we wanted to eat.

The next day Ralph again returned without getting

to see Randolph. Lucinda told Ralph that Randolph was engaged. Ralph asked about our wages, and she gave him five dollars. It wasn't our wages, but it satisfied Clutter for the time being. The five dollars lasted Clutter and Ralph about an hour, and they were broke again.

We were eating supper when I saw Freck walk by the hotel carrying his banjo. I ran to the door and called to him. He was unshaven and pretty sour-faced. We invited him to have supper with us, and he cheered up after he had some food and coffee inside him.

Freck had been hired to play his banjo with the Crescent Hotel band, but when they found out that he couldn't read music he had been fired.

Freck said, "I told them that I could play anything I heard, but that conductor wouldn't listen to me. He said he didn't have time to waste on me memorizing the music. So I told him where to go."

"What are you going to do now? Is there a band you can play with?" I asked.

"I don't know," he muttered. Then, after another coffee, he said, "Bob War, how would you like to dance for me and another feller?"

I said, "Sure!"

"Maybe we can make some loose change," he said. "Leastways, enough to get back home."

Freck told me to wait there for him. Clutter and Ralph and I had another cup of coffee. Freck returned shortly with a tall sad-faced man carrying a guitar slung over his back and a wire harness around his neck that held a harmonica. Freck introduced the guitar player to us.

"Now what we'll do is go down to the train station when the tourists come in. We'll play, and you dance for them. We'll have a Mason jar out for donations, and we'll put a dollar or two inside so the people will get the idea to give money. Now, Clutter, I would like for you to take this dollar bill and put it in the Mason jar when we finish playing. And Ralph, you put these coins into the jar. Make them rattle. Tell us how you enjoyed the music so the tourists will follow suit."

The guitar player said, "And if a policeman shows up, boy, you just grab up the Mason jar and beat it back to this hotel, you hear?"

"Why?" I said. "Is dancing against the law?"

"No, the cops don't like us making money unless they get their cut."

We walked down to the station and waited until the passenger train arrived. Carriages and taxis began lining up, and we heard the train whistle a long ways off. We set up outside, where the tourists would have to pass, and the men began playing and I began dancing.

Clutter and Ralph stood around like they didn't know us. The passengers milled around, and quite a few of them stopped to watch us. When we finished the number, Clutter shuffled forward red-faced and said in a loud voice, "I sure did like your music." He waved his dollar bill and poked it into the jar.

"Thank you," Freck said. "Thank you."

Ralph tossed his coins into the jar. "I sure did like your dancing and your music," he said.

One of the ladies stepped forward and put some money in the jar. "Thank you," Freck said. "Thank you." And he struck up another number.

Not everyone put money in the jar, but a number did. After about a half hour the station was mostly empty again. We went over to the bench and divided up the money. It really wasn't that much, but for a half hour's work it was top salary.

We went over to Basing Spring, a little park built in a half-circle design of limestone stacked to hold back the mountain. A little shelter was built there with no walls but a long pointed roof. People were resting and drinking the water. We played and danced and made a few coins.

Later, we caught the streetcar and rode over to another park by a spring, but we didn't do too good there.

We walked back to the hotel and waited around for

the next train. When we heard the train whistle, we returned to the station. We had a good crowd collected, and I was dancing up a storm, and the money was rolling into the Mason jar, when I saw a big policeman come out of the station doors. He was giving us the mean eye real good. He slapped his hand with his nightstick and headed through the crowd right toward us. I swooped up the money jar and ran like the devil was after me.

That was the end of our playing and dancing. The policeman never arrested anyone, but he gave them the what-for and read them the law. Freck was sad-faced like the last cob had been cribbed, but after supper he felt better and said he was going home, where people treated him with some respect.

The next morning, the hotel manager told Clutter at breakfast that he needed some money for the hotel room and meals: Randolph had only paid for three days. Clutter put the man off, telling him his employer would be there soon to pay him. Clutter was real cool with the man, but after the manager left he began to get worried.

After breakfast, we went up on the mountaintop to the Crescent Hotel and entered the lobby. Clutter asked for Randolph and left a message. The clerk made us wait out in the lobby.

Soon, Lucinda showed up, and I could read bad

news written all over her face. Clutter explained why we were there. And then Lucinda cut loose:

"Randolph is up there asleep. The man hasn't slept in two days. He left me alone to play poker. He wanted to come here where all the social events were, music, and dancing, and parties! And what does he do? He leaves me alone and plays poker. He has lost everything! We don't have a cent to our name! He even lost his gold watch and the Maxwell! Why, he would have bet my gold ring if he could have gotten it off my finger!"

"What are you going to do if you don't have any money?" Clutter asked. "Why me and the boys have wages due us, and the man down at the hotel wants more money."

"Money! Money!" Lucinda hissed, stamping her feet. "Well, if we are out of money, we'll just have to go get some more!"

Clutter looked down at his feet. He could see his good job just flying away.

Lucinda said to Ralph, "Go get the Maxwell, and get your things. Drive up to the backdoor, and Randolph and I will meet you there."

When we returned with the Maxwell, Lucinda and Randolph were casually strolling around the flower garden beside the drive. Lucinda had her black satchel tucked under her arm, and Randolph held the parasol to protect her from the sun. Ralph stopped alongside them. They climbed into the backseat and settled themselves.

"Drive on," Lucinda ordered.

Ralph started the car and twisted around to look at them. "Where are we going?" he asked.

"We'll go get our tents and supplies back at the cabins," Randolph said.

CHAPTER

12

I could see a smile come over Clutter's face. Tents meant we were back on the job again. Ralph opened the Maxwell up to a good speed, and we were happy again with the wind whipping past us.

Randolph and Lucinda spent most of the trip with their heads together whispering secrets. She opened her parasol and tilted it against the wind. The parasol blocked the view of Clutter and Ralph and me. But in glancing back I saw Lucinda open her black satchel beneath the parasol and remove a long-barreled Colt revolver. She checked the load and replaced the gun in the bag.

Carlo was glad to see us when we got back to the cabins. He barked and reared up on all of us and then went tearing around in circles, barking and yapping.

We got the tents and supplies out of our cabin and packed the Maxwell. Then we stood waiting around the car. Randolph and Lucinda were behind closed doors in their cabin talking.

Finally, they came out and climbed into the Maxwell. Randolph gave directions and we drove to the nearest town, where he had us wait in the car while he and Lucinda walked down the streets and looked the town over.

Then we drove on to the next town and parked and waited inside the car while Lucinda and Randolph strolled down one side of the street to the end of the town and then back down on the other side of the street. Randolph entered the bank, while Lucinda waited outside. He was only in the bank for a couple of seconds. Then he and Lucinda sauntered slowly back to the car.

"I wonder what they're doing?" Ralph said.

"It don't matter what they're doing, boys," Clutter said. "We're drawing wages just sitting here. Why that's easy work. I'm just as happy and content as I can be; I can wait here until they finish shoutin' and gather up the hymnbooks."

We made a big circuit of the area, waiting in each town while Lucinda and Randolph walked through them. It was late afternoon by the time we got back to the cabins, and we were tired and hungry.

After supper, Randolph began asking Clutter if there happened to be a road that bypassed the cabins on the way to Eureka Springs. Clutter said he knew of a different route.

Randolph said, "Why don't we go for another ride and you can show me the way." So we all piled back into the Maxwell, and Clutter had Ralph drive north two or three miles. We turned off onto a little cow path. It was slow going, but after two hours of bouncing around we came onto the main road again.

"That way is Eureka Springs, and that way is our cabin," Clutter said.

"And where does the road straight ahead go?" Randolph inquired.

"War Bonnet," Clutter answered. "It's a little village with a corn mill and a store."

"Do they have a hotel?"

"Yeah," Clutter answered.

"Good," Randolph said. "Good."

We turned back toward the cabins, and it was almost dark by the time we got there.

The next morning, we ate breakfast and Randolph informed us that he had some business in the next town. We all climbed aboard the Maxwell and Ralph drove northward.

When we approached the town, Randolph leaned forward in his seat to talk to Ralph. "I have some business to conduct," he said. "I want you to turn left up here."

Randolph had Ralph circle the block, and we parked headed south. Then he started giving orders.

"Poke, Lucinda and I have a business deal. We won't be gone but a few minutes. Leave the Maxwell running. I want to leave as soon as we get back."

"Okay," Ralph said.

"And, Bob War, you stay up there. Don't be getting down or wandering off. Stay right there. Lucinda and I will be right back."

"I'm not going anywhere," I said.

"Now, Clutter, you leave Carlo here and come with me. I want you to wait for a man for me. Bring your shotgun! Don't be leaving that shotgun in the car where someone might get hurt."

Clutter said, "Why, Mr. Randolph, the gun's not loaded."

Randolph said, "I would feel better if you just carried it with you."

"Sure," Clutter said.

"Keep that dog in the car," Randolph said as a last order.

I twisted around and watched them walk down the brick sidewalk. Randolph pointed to a spot, and Clutter stopped there and began looking around as if he were searching for someone. Randolph and Lucinda entered the bank.

"Boy, he sure is crabby today," I said.

"He's the boss!" Ralph replied drily. He held on to

Carlo's collar to keep him in the car. Carlo wanted to be with his master.

"Did you notice that they are wearing the same clothes today?" Ralph asked.

"They left their luggage at the hotel."

"Clutter said they skipped out without paying the bill," Ralph said.

Randolph and Lucinda came out of the bank walking fast. When they passed Clutter, he joined them, having to take three or four long strides to catch up.

They piled into the car and even before they were seated, Randolph ordered Ralph to start driving. The tone was forceful enough that Ralph took off fast, and we went speeding back the way we had entered town.

When we had gone a couple of blocks, I looked back over my shoulder to see a man in a business suit run out of the bank into the middle of the street. He carried a shotgun. He looked first one way and then another, and then he lifted the shotgun and pointed it right at me. I flinched, even though I knew we were out of shotgun range. But the man never fired. He lowered the weapon and ran down the street.

I didn't know it at the time, but we had just robbed a bank.

CHAPTER
13

I strongly suspicioned a bank robbery when I caught sight of Lucinda removing the Colt revolver from beneath her shawl. She opened the black satchel and slipped the gun inside. I saw the stacks of money before she got it closed. I almost had a heart attack when I realized what they had done.

I looked back to see if anyone was chasing us.

Ralph had the Maxwell running wide open at Randolph's bidding. Randolph was in a much better mood now, leaning forward and joking with Ralph and Clutter over the rushing wind.

We took the road to bypass the cabins and crossed the main road headed toward War Bonnet. It was slower going now, with steep inclines and rock-ledge roads as we wound around the mountainsides, going first up and then down inclines. Some of the curves were pretty sharp; a person couldn't go too fast on these roads.

It was getting late in the afternoon and we hadn't eaten since breakfast. Clutter wanted to stop to camp, but Randolph urged Ralph on. He told Clutter to make a list of supplies that we would need. That kept Clutter busy for a long time trying to write out a list on the rough road. He had to ask Ralph how to spell each item, and then he printed the word.

It was almost dark when we stopped at War Bonnet. It was just a little place with five or six houses perched on the hillside and a grocery store and two or three businesses. A large corn mill hung up over the river behind the tall wooden bridge. One of the buildings appeared to be a hotel; leastways, it had three stories.

Randolph ordered us to stay in the car. He took Clutter's supply list and entered the grocery store. He was gone a long time. When he returned with the groceries, he told us to go upriver and camp and return for him and Lucinda in the morning. They were going to spend the night at the hotel and eat there.

We drove into the woods, maybe a half mile. There wasn't any road or path. Clutter was hungry, so he ordered a stop.

I began to voice my suspicions about Lucinda and Randolph robbing the bank. Clutter wouldn't hear of it and began to tease me.

"Why would they be carrying pistols?" I demanded.

"Why to protect themselves, I reckon. Lots of people carry weapons. You know that!"

"What about the money I saw?"

"So? A person has to carry their money somewhere. As much as they have, I reckon a satchel would be about the right size."

"Well, what about the man who ran out of the bank with the shotgun?"

"The man didn't shoot, did he? Probably just the town crazy with a cocklebur in his pants."

"Ralph," I said pleadingly, "don't you believe me?"

"Sure," Ralph said, "but maybe Clutter's right. Strangers have strange ways."

I said, "They didn't have any money before they went into the bank, but they had stacks in that satchel when they came out."

"They made a withdrawal," Clutter said.

"Why didn't they use the Eureka Springs bank?"

"Beats me," Clutter said. "Maybe they didn't have any money there. I don't know. You guys can yap about it all you want. I just know that I am hungry. I could eat a horse. Flap your jaws while you build us a fire."

Ralph started the fire, and I busied myself dragging

up some dead wood. Clutter supervised the groceries and began preparing the food for cooking.

"I forgot to write down onions," he said. "Taters just ain't much good without onions. Bob War, why don't you run down to the store and get us some onions. You could be there and back before I get the taters peeled."

I protested, but he gave me a couple of coins and told me to go. I walked to the lights of the village.

I entered the grocery store and picked up four big onions and had just paid for them when a stout woman dressed in calico rushed into the store.

"Did you hear about the marshal arresting them strangers?" she said to the storekeeper.

When the storekeeper said no, the woman spilled out everything she knew. "Borden told me that he sent for the marshal the minute the couple signed the register. Said he recognized the names as having skipped out on paying the hotel bill at the Crescent. Real fancy dressers, he said. When he saw the name, he said, 'That'll be five dollars' cash money for the room,' and the man just slapped down five dollars. Borden took his money. The marshal and Ben Pauley went upstairs and arrested them. They took a revolver off the man. Armed he was. I wonder how they'll like spending the night in that rock shed. Won't be as fancy as the Crescent, but it won't cost as much. They made two mistakes as I see it: one was staying at the

Crescent to begin with, and the second was skipping out without paying."

I slid on out the door and broke into a dead run for the camp. I was winded and huffed and puffed as I told about Lucinda and Randolph being arrested.

Clutter said, "Ain't nothing to worry about. They'll just take them to Eureka Springs and make them pay the hotel bill. Ain't nothing to worry about."

"The lady said the marshal took a gun from Randolph, but she didn't say anything about Lucinda's pistol. What if Lucinda gets mad and shoots one of them?"

"Nonsense!" Clutter said. "We're going to eat our supper and get a good night's sleep."

We gobbled down our supper after it was cooked. We were real hungry. Then we talked by the campfire. I kept saying that Lucinda and Randolph were bank robbers. I suggested that we all resign our positions and take off right then and there. Clutter wouldn't hear of it.

I gave up talking after that. I got out our blankets and settled down by the fire. Clutter wasn't his usual lazy self, but started to pace back and forth. Finally, he said, "I think I'll mosey down to the village and nose around."

Neither Ralph nor I said anything. Clutter tied Carlo up so he wouldn't follow him, and then he got out his shotgun, loaded it, and slipped some extra shells into his pocket.

We could hear him moving away from the camp and then nothing but the night sounds and the sound of the river.

Clutter roused us out of a deep sleep. He told us we were going to get Randolph and Lucinda out of jail. He started gathering up the equipment.

"Come on, boys," he said. "We have to get the Maxwell packed."

"Why?" I asked.

Clutter kept on working. "Well, first off they ain't no bank robbers. Randolph explained that. He had had a large amount of money wired to the Wellsville bank because they did business with his father's coal mine. You see, his daddy is involved in this lawsuit with another big company. And they laid papers on Randolph to be a witness against his own daddy. So Randolph ran. He didn't want to testify against his daddy. That's the reason he and Lucinda were out here in the sticks. He's just hiding out until the trial's over. He said if the police check his name, why he'll be taken back for sure. Said the other company had a bunch of detectives out looking for him high and low."

"So that's who the skeletonman is," Ralph said. "A detective! Well, I'll be hornswoggled! Who would have dreamed?"

It all made sense to me, I guess, all sleepy-eyed and tired. We collapsed camp and loaded the Maxwell. Ralph idled the car real quiet back to the village, and Clutter just pointed out directions to him silently.

We backed up to a little rock shed built next to one of the buildings, and Clutter jumped out and attached ropes to the barred window.

He gave me the loose ends of two ropes and told me in a whisper that when we pulled the bars loose I was to give the ropes a hard tug to loose the slipknots. That way we wouldn't be dragging anything.

Clutter got into the Maxwell, and Ralph gave it the gas. We shot forth and bang! We came to a stop. The wheels started spinning. Ralph reversed gears and backed up and took another shot at it. And wham! The whole middle of the wall collapsed and a big black hole appeared.

Randolph and Lucinda came scrambling out of the hole and piled into the Maxwell. Voices were shouting now, and lights were appearing. Ralph swung the Maxwell around and headed for the bridge. I tugged at the ropes but couldn't get them to slip. We were dragging the iron bars and making a big ruckus.

Clutter came climbing over the front seat and stood between Lucinda and Randolph. He took the ropes from me and gave a big tug. The ropes slipped free of their knot, and Clutter released the ends. The bars came to rest on the bridge.

121

By daybreak, Clutter had us so deep in the timber, we figured no one could find us. We were back in Missouri. We stopped near a little stream, and Clutter pitched a tent for Lucinda and Randolph while Ralph and I cooked breakfast.

After we had eaten, we all settled down for some sleep. Lucinda and Randolph went into their tent, and we just sacked out on a blanket under a tree.

The sun was pretty high when I awoke. Ralph was already up and busy tinkering with the Maxwell. Clutter woke up and looked around like he was trying to remember where he was. He got up from the blanket and picked up his shotgun.

"I think I'll go up on that rise to see if anyone is around."

"I'll go with you," I said. I got my rifle and we walked to the hilltop. Clutter kept Carlo on a leash so he wouldn't go to hunting and bark. When we got to the hilltop, Clutter gave me his shotgun and he climbed up a tall tree. He stayed up for a long time looking the country over.

Finally, he climbed down, I handed him his shotgun, and we returned to camp. Lucinda and Randolph were up now, so I stirred up the fire and started dinner.

Ralph said, "Clutter, can you help me carry up some wood?"

That was my job. Clutter couldn't think of a good

excuse to get out of work, so he grudgingly followed Ralph off into the timber.

I knew something was up. Ralph was getting Clutter off to talk in private. They were gone a long time. Each had an armload of dead sticks when they returned. They were pretty quiet.

Randolph noticed something amiss. As we ate dinner, he told us how loyal we were and how we had saved his daddy's coal mine by helping him and Lucinda get out of jail. He bragged on us a lot.

After dinner, Clutter told me to stack up some more wood for the night. I just hurried right on out into the timber because I knew either Ralph or Clutter would soon be right behind to tell me something.

It was Ralph, and he was madder than a wet hen on a long-legged June bug.

"You're right, Warren. They're both a couple of bank robbers, and that skeletonman who we keep running into used to be their partner. His name is Clarence. They double-crossed Clarence, and now he's out to kill them. That's why they're hiding out here in the boonies."

"How did you find out, Ralph?"

"I was packing the wheel bearings and had crawled under the Maxwell to check the undercarriage, when Lucinda came out to the car, poking around in the backseat. I didn't want to crawl out while she was in the car, so I just stayed quiet where I was. Then along came Randolph, and they stood there making plans for their next robbery."

"What are we going to do?"

"Clutter wants to wait until the middle of the night, and we'll just walk off and leave them here."

"I'm for that idea," I said.

"Clutter will package some food for us tonight. You keep your rifle next to you because when Clutter says go, we're going to go."

I got to thinking about Ma's sheets. I wasn't going to leave without those sheets no matter what. So after we were back in camp for a while, I wandered over to the Maxwell and looked in the backseat. There, on the floor under everything else, were my sheets, still wrapped in the brown paper. I thought I would slide the package out for easy grabbing tonight, but Randolph came over when he saw me fooling about the Maxwell.

Instead, I dragged out the carpetbag with Ralph's and my clothes. I opened it up and was tossing clothing around when Randolph got to me.

"I thought now would be a good time to wash out a few things," I said. I grabbed a bar of lye soap and headed for the stream. Thinking that he might nosey about to watch me, I tossed the clothes in the stream and gave them a scrubbing and spread them out on bushes to dry.

When it got dark, we all went to bed. I couldn't

rest. I listened for Clutter to give us a sign. A long time passed, and I finally heard a faint noise as Clutter picked up his blanket and gun and moved off toward the stream. Ralph nudged me, and I picked up my blanket and rifle and edged slowly over to the Maxwell. I put down the blanket and rifle and leaned over and quietly moved things around until I could get to my sheets. I put both hands on the package so the paper wouldn't rustle and lifted the sheets out of the car.

I got my rifle and blanket and slipped off to the stream, where Ralph and Clutter were packing our clothes in a pair of Ralph's overalls to make a bundle. We sneaked off, following Clutter.

He headed due north, toward home. After we cleared the hilltop, we stepped out at a pretty fast pace. We walked all through the night. The next morning we cooked our breakfast and turned in for some sleep.

In the late afternoon, we started out, again walking north. Clutter shot a couple of squirrels Carlo treed for us, and that evening we had squirrel for supper. We rested a spell before we started walking again.

We camped beneath a small outcropping of rock near a clear stream. We cooked the last of our food. All we had left was salt and flour and some baking soda. I went to sleep as soon as I hit the blanket. We were dog tired from walking.

It was late morning when I opened my eyes. Something had awakened me. I felt uneasy and scared for some reason, and I just lay there looking at the grass and listening. Then I moved my head real slow and let my gaze run up across the meadow to the hilltop. There was a horseman staring down at our camp.

Even from this distance, I could recognize the skeletonman.

CHAPTER

❧ 14 ❧

The horseman did not move, just remained frozen against the morning sky. I didn't dare make any movement. Perhaps the brown blankets blended in with the landscape. Maybe he couldn't make out what we were at this distance. A long time passed before the rider turned the horse and moved off across the hilltop. I lost sight of him in the trees.

I didn't waste any time. I roused Clutter and Ralph, and we were on the move in a hurry. We went in the opposite direction that the skeletonman had taken, following the stream. After a mile or so, we swung north again and really made time. By noon we were plumb wore out, tired and hungry and dying of thirst.

I begged for a rest, and Clutter pointed out that after we got into the trees we would be headed downhill. Perhaps some water would be at the bottom of the hill. We moved on across the open area. We were

127

almost to the trees when we came to a road. We looked down it both ways and crossed it and moved into the trees.

We found water at the bottom of the hill just like Clutter said we would. A wide shallow creek meandered through the valley. We threw down our bundles and guns and bellied down to the stream to drink. The water was clear and cold and tasted good.

"By George, that sure hits the spot," Clutter said, and then he sucked in his breath.

He had heard a horse stamp his feet downstream. Clutter stared in the direction of the sound.

I moved back from the water and looked downstream for the horse. I bent down and picked up my rifle.

"Stand right there," a harsh voice commanded behind us.

We spun around, and there was the skeletonman standing about a stone's throw away. He had that long-barreled revolver in his bony hand, and he had it lined up on us. He had taken us by surprise, and we just stood frozen. I cocked back the hammer of my rifle, and when Clutter heard its metallic click, he broke for a tree.

"Scatter, boys! Scatter!" he yelled.

The man fired. The slug knocked a chunk of bark off the tree Clutter chose for cover. The second shot splashed in the water.

I bellied down behind an old log that had washed down the stream during high water. I lay facedown, pushed up against the decaying wood. I waited for another shot. None came, so I risked poking my head up over the log.

The skeletonman was walking toward us at a fast pace. He was watching the tree Clutter was behind. Clutter broke cover and darted to another tree. The skeletonman fired, and Clutter broke into a run toward me. He took about six steps and dove for the bank of the stream.

The man fired again, and water splashed about thirty feet from Clutter. The man was a poor shot. Clutter was up, running to me again, and dove behind my log. He rolled up against me.

"That's four shots," he hissed out. He was breathing hard. "One more shot to go! No fool would ride a horse out in this brush with a live shell under the hammer."

I poked my head back up for another look.

"Shoot next to him, Bob War. Scare him into using his last shot."

I lined up my rifle and brought the man into my sights.

"Unless he's some sort of idiot he'll only have five rounds in that six-shooter," Clutter reasoned.

I moved the man out of my sight and tried to chip some bark off a tree next to him. I squeezed the trigger, and the man flinched.

He fired in our direction.

"Let's get him, boys!" Clutter yelled and scrambled over the log. He charged the man. I stood up and dug in my pocket for another shell.

The skeletonman leveled his gun on Clutter, and Plow! The slicker had six cartridges in the pistol. I thought Clutter was dead. He stumbled, fell, and then was up running again.

The man turned to run from Clutter and took a step or two. He glanced back and saw Clutter was too close. He turned and threw his empty revolver. He was more accurate throwing the gun than he was shooting. The pistol thudded off Clutter's chest, and then Clutter was on top of the man.

He turned his body and threw Clutter away from him. The two men began swinging roundhouses at each other as fast as they could. They looked like two berserk windmills gone haywire. Very few of the blows were landing, and they weren't hurting anything.

Ralph came rushing in and tackled the man's leg. Ralph's weight took the man down, and Clutter jumped on top of him, flailing away with his fists. Ralph clung to the man's leg, and the man kicked about with his free foot as he thrashed around. Carlo barked and circled the fighters.

I finally fished a bullet out of my pocket. I ejected the spent shell and inserted the new one. I ran up to the fighters and tapped the man on the head with my rifle.

"That's enough," I yelled. "Stop it!"

He grabbed at the rifle barrel, and I jerked it back. He renewed swinging his fists and kicking out with his foot.

"You kick my brother again," I said, "and I'll shoot you for sure." I tapped his head with the rifle just to make my point.

The man stopped fighting then. He stared up at me with mean, dead eyes. I took a step back.

Clutter put his elbow into the man's chest to balance himself and reached his right arm back to his belt to extract his skinning knife. Clutter put the knife to the man's throat.

"One move out of you, pardner, and I'll slit you from here to Texas!"

Ralph took over then. He took the man's belt and tied his hands behind his back.

"There now," Ralph said. "Why are you following us around? What have Warren and I ever done to you except try to scare you at the bridge? I would call everything even, wouldn't you? What do you want with us?"

"Answer the boy," Clutter said.

"You're with Randolph, aren't you?"

"He must be Clarence," I said to Ralph.

"I reckon," Ralph said.

Clutter picked up the man's empty revolver, and then he sat down to rest. He was still puffing from the fight.

Ralph went downstream and found Clarence's horse and led him back to us. Ralph stripped off the saddle, removed the bridle, and slapped the horse across the rump to get him to run away.

Ralph said to Clarence, "We're going to rest a while, and then I'll set you free. We have your gun and you're afoot now, so I guess you won't be bothering us no more. And as you can see, we're not with Randolph. We left them when we found out he was a bank robber."

Clarence started to say something but didn't. He cleared his throat and looked away.

We had been resting for maybe five minutes when we heard the Maxwell. It was up at the top of the hill somewhere, hidden by the trees. We saw sunlight flash off the windshield, and we spotted the car coming down the hill.

Randolph was driving and Lucinda was standing up, pointing one hand at us and gripping the windshield with the other. I moved off behind one of the big trees and squatted down with my back to it.

"There's Clarence," Lucinda said, and she yelled at

him. Clarence called her a bad name, and they shouted at one another until Randolph got the Maxwell stopped next to my tree. He got out and ran around the car. Randolph shouted in Clarence's face.

The three of them really exchanged foul names with each other. If words could be weapons they would have all been sliced up pretty bad. Finally, Lucinda wore down, and she turned her wrath on us.

"Where's that little sneak thief that stole my money?" she shouted.

"We didn't steal any money," Clutter said.

"You did too!" she insisted. She bent down and came up with her revolver. She pointed the long-barreled Colt at Clutter. "You did too! You did too!" And she shook the pistol at him.

She realized the pistol wasn't cocked and, holding the gun in both hands, she cocked back the hammer. "I want my money. Bring me those sheets. Bring me those sheets!"

"I'll get them," Ralph said. "Just be careful with that gun. The sheets are right over here."

I could picture her getting Ma's sheets and she and Randolph driving off with them. I had gone through too much to lose Ma's sheets now. I crawfished over to the Maxwell and stepped up onto the running board. She felt my weight on the car, and as her pistol came up, I tapped her upside the head with my rifle.

The pistol fired, and she pitched forward over the side of the car and somersaulted onto the ground. She fell flat on her back with a thud.

"Land's sake. He's killed her," Clutter said.

Clutter and Randolph gathered her up, and Clutter rubbed her wrists while Randolph fanned her. Carlo whined and tried to nose in to lick her face. Even Clarence came over with concern written on his dead face. Lucinda began to moan.

"You could have killed her," Ralph said, scolding me. "Everything would have been okay. I was going to give her the sheets."

"Not my sheets, you weren't," I said. I took the package of sheets from Ralph and picked up Lucinda's revolver and moved away from them. I fished out my pocketknife and cut the strips to the package and unwrapped the paper.

Hidden in between my sheets were stacks of money. At the sight of the money, Randolph let go of Lucinda and started toward me. I pointed Lucinda's pistol at him. "No!" I said.

He stopped.

"I didn't know the money was in here," I apologized.

Randolph said, "She hid it there so I couldn't find it. She didn't want me gambling."

"Where are my other two sheets?" I asked.

"They're in her satchel," Randolph said.

I went to the Maxwell and pulled out the satchel. Inside were my sheets. I took them out and placed them with the others. Then I put the money in the satchel and tossed it to Randolph.

"There's your money," I said. "Now leave us alone."

Clutter patted Lucinda's hands. "You're going to be just fine, ma'am. Real fine. We're going to leave you now."

Ralph and Clutter gathered their gear, and I repacked the sheets and tied the package secure. We were ready to leave.

Clutter said to Randolph, "You still owe us some wages."

Randolph smiled and took some bills out of the satchel and handed them to Clutter.

"Thank you," Clutter said. "So long. Bye, ma'am."

We crossed the stream and started across the valley. I looked back over my shoulder for what I hoped was my last look at the strangers. They were arguing again.

Then I saw movement up on the hill. I stopped and turned around for a better look. A bunch of horsemen were coming down the hill. They were spread out in a skirmish line.

"Look!" I said to Clutter.

"It's a posse! Let's make tracks, boys, or we're in deep trouble."

He took off like a scared rabbit with Ralph and me right at his heels. Suddenly, there were horsemen in front of us coming at a gallop. Clutter turned abruptly downstream. Ralph and I followed him at a dead run. I looked back to see the horsemen surround the Maxwell. Randolph stood with his hands on his hips, and Lucinda was waving her arms around. She was probably giving the posse a lot of harsh words.

We made for the timber and lost ourselves from the men. We ran the ridges darting out and around branches and shrubs.

We ran for a long time. It felt like my chest was a hot furnace. Clutter was gasping for air, but kept on running. We came down off the ridge into a long hollow, and Clutter stopped running and began a fast walk.

"Lordy," he gasped, "I can't run no further."

We went marching Indian file right on down the hollow. We almost walked by the horseman before we saw him. He sat easy on a big roan, and his Winchester was pointed right at us. We stopped dead still.

"Lay down that shotgun," he said to Clutter. Clutter just let it drop to the ground. "Now that pistol, real easy." And Clutter pulled Clarence's revolver from his belt and dropped it.

"Now you, son," he said to me.

I let the butt of the rifle down to the ground and made the barrel fall away from the horseman. Then I slowly removed Lucinda's pistol and placed it on the ground.

"Move away from the weapons, boys!"

We did as he said.

"Just set yourselves down for a rest. It might be a long wait," the man said. He raised his Winchester and fired three single shots to let the posse know he had found us.

It was a long time before the posse arrived, and it was after dark before they locked us up in jail.

CHAPTER

15

"So that's how we came to be here, your honor. That's how we met Clarence. Ralph and I didn't do him any harm. And the three of us were just working for Randolph for wages."

The judge peered down at me over his eyeglasses and screwed his jaw around two or three times before he spoke.

He said, "In light of this testimony and sworn deposition of other witnesses, this court is going to release the three of you. However, this court cautions you-all against the consequences of consorting with criminals. I hope you have learned your lesson from this experience."

"Yes, sir," I said. "Thank you, sir."

The judge rose and started to leave.

"Your Honor, sir," I said. "What about my sheets?"

"Ah, yes, your sheets," the judge said, and he

looked over at the sheriff who nodded his agreement. "Yes, you may take possession of your sheets."

"And my rifle?"

The judge frowned.

Clutter nudged me and whispered, "Ask him for Carlo and my shotgun."

The judge said, "Give them back all their belongings."

The sheriff took off the handcuffs and shackles, and we went back down to the jail and collected our things. We stepped out into the sunshine free men. It sure felt good to be out of that cell.

Clutter said, "We'll go get Carlo, and then we'll shake the dust of this town."

"Sounds good to me," Ralph said. "The sooner we leave the better for me. I just wish we had the Maxwell to go home in and not have to walk."

"Well, I've got an idea, boys," Clutter says. "Let's hop us a freight train. Why should we walk when we can ride!"

"A freight train!" Ralph said. "Boy, I've never ridden on a freight train before."

I sighed and tightened my grip on the package of sheets and hurried my pace to keep up with them.